Wentworth-By-The-Sea, 1969

Wentworth-By-The-Sea, 1969

A Novel

SUSAN CHAPMAN MELANSON

To order additional copies of this book, contact:
Xlibris Corporation
1-888-7-XLIBRIS
www.Xlibris.com
Orders@Xlibris.com

Contents

To my husband, Art, who inspired me
to get it all down on paper before I began to forget.

"WE WALKED ON THE BEACH BESIDE THAT OLD HOTEL.
THEY'RE TEARING IT DOWN NOW BUT IT'S JUST AS WELL.
THIS IS THE TIME TO REMEMBER,
'CAUSE IT WILL NOT LAST FOREVER."
BILLY JOEL

CHAPTER 1

The Arrival

Hiram, Ohio, April, 1969

I had to maneuver a slalom course between a backgammon game, a pedicure-in-progress and a forest of coffee cups to get to the television. The Late Night News had just flashed a brief story about a raging hotel fire on the New England coast–not much interest to a dorm of college girls in the middle of Ohio–except to me! I was watching my summer employment going up in flames.

I was counting on waitressing at one of the last of the grand hotels. I needed a respite from the uncertainty of life in 1969. I needed a change of pace–new activity, new people, a new setting, and maybe a new romance. For a year and a half I felt like the weight of the world had rested squarely upon my young shoulders. Since returning to college I had jumped headlong into the eye of the storm that seemed to be raging on most campuses. We felt indignation, anger and frustration over political processes and politicians that had allowed the War in Vietnam to linger on so long. I became vocal at campus rallies and participated in demonstrations in Cleveland, New York and Washington DC. All of us knew we were being watched. A friend from high school worked for the FBI and had actually seen a file with my name on it. But the greatest fear I felt was fear of the local draft board that held the fate of my younger brother in their hands. Despite my efforts to make a difference Bobby Kennedy and Martin Luther King were assassinated. Despite my efforts the War in Vietnam escalated. And, finally, despite everything and anything I could do, my younger brother became a US Marine. I had been in the streets of Chicago during the 1968 Democratic Convention and I had returned home emotionally battered, drained of my idealism and very, very tired. I needed a light-hearted summer to restore my youth, my sense of humor, and my ability to play. I wanted to forget Vietnam, the mace in Chicago and my disillusionment with the American System. I had chosen Wentworth-By-The-Sea as my retreat from reality. It exuded Victorian formality and charm and grace. I had hoped that the 95-year-old resort, along with the ever-healing ocean would regenerate my senses, my values and my optimism. And there it was burning bright and spectacular on the Late Night News.

One week later I received a letter from the James Barker Smiths, owners of the hotel, stating that a business-as-usual attitude was being assumed. The employees' dormitories were the only buildings destroyed and alternative housing was being arranged. (There was no mention of the watchman who lost his life in the blaze.) And so my summer plans were saved!

The approach to Wentworth-By-The-Sea was breathtaking.

The resort was the main attraction in the quaint coastal village of New Castle, New Hampshire, a town comprised entirely of islands linked by bridges. The massive white façade crowned by red roofs and towers loomed near the mouth of the Piscataqua River. Glimpses of the Grand

Lady could be seen from a great distance but as one rounded the bend by the golf course, just over the drawbridge, she towered, ageless, formal and proud.

My alternative quarters were in Colonial Cottage, a misleading name for a large, drafty, white house that a dozen waitresses called home.

My roommate for the summer greeted me with a sunny Sarasota drawl. Mandy was tall and willowy with waist length blond hair and broad, fashionable glasses. She was clutching a 500-page novel as she met me at the door. She had a contagious sparkle and I liked her immediately. Three of us were assigned to Room 5, a bright second floor room with a picture postcard view of the rocky cove behind the hotel.

We were wrestling the last of my suitcases into the room when a crashing door heralded the arrival of Babs, our across-the-hall neighbor. Babs was a whirlwind of thick sandy hair, long tan legs and flashing eyes. She bounded into our room to introduce herself and vent her anger. Her afternoon water skiing date had not gone well! Breathless from the short jog up from the Ski Shack she spun out of her dripping bathing suit and tugged at her hairbrush. Babs' vocabulary, especially when she was as livid as she was that day, could rival any sailor. Soon she huffed out her story.

There were two broad-shouldered Irish brothers who lived locally and fraternized closely with the hotel crew. There was always booming laughter and intimidating innuendos when they were around. They had an unnerving way of sizing up the new crop of waitresses and Clark Kent would have been proud of their x-ray vision. Even more unnerving was the fact that the brothers could pass for one another when they weren't side by side. Babs hadn't known that. In fact she hadn't known that there were two of them. The evening before, Babs had met Chip at a party, and they hit it off so well that she hadn't come home that night. Chip arranged the Ski Shack date at which time Babs came face to face with his brother. She spent a fun-filled afternoon with the brother and as she left, came face to face with Chip. The brothers got a great chuckle out of her disbelief. But she was only one in a series of victims of the brothers' identity switch. Mandy and I were trying hard not to laugh.

Going downstairs for one last suitcase, Mandy and I bumped into (quite literally), an embracing couple. They were college sweethearts who only had eyes for each other. I figured that somewhere between his Weejuns and her Pappagallo tiptoes there had to be an Izod alligator. Introductions were unnecessary–they were in a world of their own.

Introductions, however, were warm and abundant outside on the porch.

Backed up to the porch was the annex to Colonial Cottage: a mobile home housing another half dozen waitresses. Bubbles was an old-timer and returned year after year. She was middle-aged, well padded and her nickname suited her. She was the one who came up with the name Rock-A-Bye Trailer. Another of the Rock-A-Bye girls was Cher. Cher could have been a model. She had flawless skin and a mane of shiny brunette hair that cascaded to her waist.

Colonial Cottage had an interesting cast of characters and my head was spinning, trying to take in every detail of my new world.

Mandy pointed out that it was time for dinner.

We headed through the Pine Woods that separated Colonial Cottage from the vast expanse of hotel parking lot that lay beyond. As we emerged from the woods I felt like royal trumpeters should have heralded our arrival.

The Wentworth stood vast and white against the sky, a token of a dying resort lifestyle. Between the woods and the hotel the asphalt was still setting up. That was where the ill-fated dorms had been.

We skirted the sticky parking lot and passed a converted chicken coop which was yet another makeshift dorm. Colonial Cottage was looking cozier by the moment.

As we got closer to the back of the hotel, the romantic first impression gave way to the noise and smells of the kitchens. We climbed the steep, worn steps to The Zoo. All employees, except the upper echelon, took their meals in a special dining room aptly called The Zoo. It consisted of a cafeteria style serving area and a barracks line-up of wooden tables and mis-matched chairs. The Zoo Cook had prepared a "sumptuous" meal of mashed potatoes, sausages and gravy. The gravy had a unique flavor that became familiar over the course of the season. It was rumored that the Zoo Cook used the same horrible beef bone over and over again from May to October. Dessert was in a gigantic steel bowl, butterscotch pudding bathtub style.

Mandy and I slid our trays onto the table across from an unlikely couple who didn't seem to be able to eat without as much body contact as possible. Kirsten was a tall Scandinavian girl, solidly built and well endowed. Her companion was Robert, perched at her elbow like a tiny bird. Despite his small stature he was very self-confident—almost excessively so—immaculately groomed, he held his head high with a regal, almost haughty air.

Our attention was quickly drawn away from the big blond girl and her birdman, to the din at the next table. A domestic squabble! The couple of the year (last year) had been the talk of the Wentworth when they had tied the knot and headed south for the winter. Their one-year of wedded bliss was apparently coming to a stormy end. Leslie was a strong-willed, hard-working, intelligent girl who, in a moment of silly passion had teamed up with Zack. Zack was shiftless, lazy and a professional party animal, but he had charisma! There was no doubt about the charisma!

Mandy and I dissected and ingested as many sausages as we dared and cleared our trays. In a tiny windowless cubbyhole off The Zoo I checked in with Mary Hart, Director of Personnel. Miss Hart was a fixture at the Wentworth and represented the best interests of the "proper society" the Wentworth was famous for servicing. After the required paperwork was completed, we gathered with the rest of the staff for the Grand Tour.

Beyond The Zoo was a maze of corridors that led to storerooms, a distant coffee shop, the lounge, the Avenida Terrace and other public rooms. A vast chasm at the other end of The Zoo became the kitchens. The noise of the ovens firing up, the ancient ceiling fans creaking and cooks yelling made my head throb. In time I got used to the noise. I never got used to the heat. We were promised an in-depth tour of the kitchens at a later time and proceeded on to the Main Dining Room. This would become my second home that summer.

The Main Dining Room was a spooky place with all the tables shrouded. Some of the windows were still shuttered against winter gales. There was a smell of dampness, age and mustiness. But even through the trappings of winter storage, the Main Dining Room was elegant. It had high, beamed ceilings with carved moldings, massive pillars, ornate cornices, and graceful crystal and brass chandeliers.

During The Season, certain areas of the hotel would be off-limits to the dining room staff, but before those limitations were imposed Mandy wanted me to experience the Front Lobby and we slipped away from the others. The Front Lobby was indeed the heart of the hotel. Carved paneling and tall, gilt mirrors had witnessed generations of the wealthy and the would-be-wealthy coming and going. An ancient iron grating guarded the News Nook, beside which was a tiny cubbyhole that was the Wentworth-By-The-Sea post office with its very own zip code. French doors topped with leaded glass transoms led the way from the Front Lobby into a formal parlor on one side and a circular room straight ahead which was referred to as the Foyer. On the ceiling of the Foyer angels and light blue clouds had been painted. Curling gracefully above us was the distinctive Wentworth trademark, a graceful sea nymph astride a stylized dolphin. Mandy and I wandered about, admiring ornate fireplaces, antique writing tables and panoramic views of the harbor. The historical feel of the place was seeping into my soul. We spoke of the international dignitaries who had come to hash out the details of the Russo-Japanese Treaty in 1905 at the urging of Teddy Roosevelt. Neither of us knew much about Russo-Japanese history, but with Teddy Roosevelt involved the treaty talks must have been a monumental event.

A broad veranda wrapped around the hotel overlooking The Ship. The Ship was a wooden fantasy, housing a ballroom/movie theater, lounge, swimming pools with their cabanas and a couple of shops. Beyond The Ship a long pier extended into the harbor. At the tip of the pier was a small red-roofed building known as The Ski Shack.

This was rumored to be the private playground of the owners' son. This was also the scene of Babs' recent folly.

This was the universe into which I had chosen to immerse myself for the next three months. I savored the elegance and the tradition. A "Town and Country" magazine lay on a mahogany end table and had an advertisement on the back that drew our attention. It urged: "Flash across the summer scene like a shooting star. Crowd a thousand exciting things into the short bright months." So Mandy and I decided that this would be a fitting motto for the summer of 1969. Summer was, after all, not so much a season as a state of mind.

CHAPTER 2

Exploration

Official starting time was 8:00 AM the next morning, but until that hour it was Party Time! The sun set and a flurry of activity at Colonial Cottage set major transformations into motion. The showers were in constant use and enough hair dryers, electric rollers and make-up mirrors were plugged in, that the circuit breakers had to be re-set three times. A stereo blared: "…This is the dawning of the Age of Aquarius!"

Within a half hour the first string was out the door headed for Ladd's Pioneer Lounge to mix, mingle, drink and dance. Cher and her UNH boyfriend urged me to join them, but I decided to save Ladd's for another time.

The second string was waiting in the wings. These girls were bound for the Ski Shack. Babs' recent tale of mortification was reason enough not to go there! Oddly enough Babs opted to join that group. A masochist, that girl!

The rest of us headed for Portsmouth. Portsmouth was an enchanting city. The graceful white spire of the church in Market Square was silhouetted against the sky and ancient cobblestones held secrets of by-gone days when sea captains and their ladies descended from their white-columned mansions. In 1969 there was an air of rejuvenation about the city but the restoration was just beginning. There were some areas with blocks of deteriorating residences, tacky storefronts and rotting wharves, but people with vision were predicting what they could become. History, charm and possibilities melted together to make Portsmouth irresistible.

Our destination that evening was Gilley's, a trolley-like vehicle that looked like it had rolled off the cover of "Wind In The Willows". Each evening it rattled into Market Square and set up for business. From the worn grill Gilley himself served up the region's best hot dogs and chili. His wagon was there every evening and a 2:00 AM flurry of business was not uncommon.

After our second supper at Gilley's, Mandy and I wandered around Market Square getting our bearings. We noted where the Greyhound Bus Station was in case we needed to make a quick getaway; Newbury's Department Store for shoe polish and pantyhose; a Laundromat in a side alley; a couple of trash-and-treasure shops that warranted a second look; and Richardson's. In Richardson's, one could buy beer, wine, or the newest rage, Champale. Also, Hostess Cupcakes, beef jerky and those addictive cheese things that make your lips orange for two days afterwards. Mandy and I split a package of Twinkies and strolled through the soft, warm evening.

The next morning, after a hasty Zoo breakfast, the 1969 Main Dining Room staff assembled for their first review by Maitre'd Leo J. Ruth.

About one-quarter of the Main Dining Room staff were regulars, returning year after year. The oldest was Millie who was rumored to be 92. Clusters of the hotel regulars sat lackadaisically waiting for Mr. Ruth. Younger girls stood fidgeting nervously.

Presently, the etched glass doors at the front of the Main Dining Room opened and everyone hopped to their feet. Leo Ruth had arrived with Walter Polak, his assistant.

Mr. Ruth was dressed in a black suit–impeccable even at 8 o'clock in the morning. His massive, formal figure moved slowly, deliberately, down the aisle, examining every detail of his domain. He stopped in front of us and without a word we instinctively fell into line. His eyes moved up the line–critical, inquisitive, summing us up in a glance.

He folded his massive hands behind his back and began to pace. He was ruler here, there was no doubt about that and he was asserting his power. In the hotel line of command, the next in line below Mr. Ruth and his assistant were his three hostesses. I half expected them to drop to their knees as he passed.

"Leo Ruth is my name. I am your Sovereign!" I don't know whether he said it or simply radiated the message. We all understood it. With a simple gesture he delegated his power to the three hostesses and they took over the initial session. It was beneath him to expound on the policies and procedures of the Wentworth or instruct us in the fine art of fingerbowls or serving Chateau Briand.

The days that followed were spent bringing the Main Dining Room to life, assembling it as it had been done every season for almost a century. Crisp white table linens came out of closets and stacks of napkins had to be hand-folded precisely as they always had been, different colors for different meals. Wooden boxes were carried out filled with the hotel silverware, each piece engraved with a simple "W". The silver had to be polished. Service plates were hauled up from chambers beneath the hotel, each glazed with an aerial view of Wentworth-By-The-Sea in shades of green. Salt cellars had to be filled, antique sugar bowls unpacked and everything made spotless.

One morning we were fitted for our uniforms. We went in shifts to a window-less cubbyhole where two jolly seamstresses presided over racks and racks of uniforms for everyone on the property from the waitresses, to the bellhops, to the gardeners. We left the cubbyhole laden with an entire wardrobe of uniforms.

In the kitchen we learned the distinct jurisdictions of each cook and what each one did under the skilled orchestration of Chef Robert Horne. Chef Horne held the power of a sea captain–the power of life or death over all of his crew. He had been hand picked and wooed by the management for the skills and experience he brought to the Wentworth. He was responsible for the five star food service rating.

There were also specific fry cooks, sous chefs, and broiler cooks.

One of the sub-chefs was Fletch, the short, solidly built less-than-benevolent despot of the Salad Room. It was rumored that the lump under his white uniform was a small firearm. We envisioned his pulling a sawed off shotgun out of his pant leg should any misguided waitress garnish a melon wrong.

Neil was in charge of oatmeal. And it was very fine oatmeal, but that was all he seemed to do–or want to do. His goal that summer was to party. And if he liked it, he was considering partying as a lifetime career.

One of the dishwashers had earned himself the name "Bullet Man". In hushed whispers we heard the tale of a shoot-out gone bad several years before. Bullet Man had a noticeable limp and supposedly carried a souvenir of the event in his left thigh.

Alv was an institution at the Wentworth and had been there as long as anyone could remember. He had limited functions due to his habitual intoxication, so his job that particular summer was to maneuver the garbage cans from the food preparation area to the loading dock where the dumpsters sat. Each summer there was at least one instance of Alv loosing his balance and falling into the dumpster along with bushels of raw, ripe garbage. He had long since learned that struggling was futile and he usually fell asleep (or passed out) in his mushy resting place, until Red came along and rescued him.

Red was a big teddy bear of a man who helped out wherever he was needed. He was the one who would remember a waitress's birthday with candles and a song, send hot soup to the dorm if a girl was under the weather; or loan a bus boy car muffler money when disaster struck. Red had a heart as big as all outdoors, but his eyes were noticeably sad. I thought he might have a secret history but I never asked.

Mr. Riediger was the Food and Beverage Manager. He was in charge of ordering and stocking everything. He was an inventory wizard and the financial success of the food service end of the hotel operation rested, in a large part, on his abilities. We all suspected that he had a first name, but no one dared contemplate it, much less use it. Mr. Riediger looked like he had stepped straight out of a Roaring 20's movie. He wore a tweed jacket, wire-rim spectacles and slicked back hair. We always wondered whether he knew Al Capone.

So many faces–So many names–So many duties–My job was to learn my role and mesh with the others. That's how the whole operation worked.

CHAPTER 3

Party At the Stables

After the long hours that first week, a major party was in order. Such a party spontaneously materialized at the Stables.

Within walking distance of the Main Hotel was a wooded peninsula that jutted into the harbor and there the Clam Bake Area and Stables hugged the shore.

Horse back riding had long since been dropped from the list of attractions at the Wentworth. The stalls had been converted into booths and the broad barn doors could be slid aside to allow the ocean breezes in. The Clam Bake Area and Stables were far enough away from the rest of the complex that a substantial stereo set-up could be turned up to peak volume without Security or the New Castle constable stepping in.

Robert, the little birdman, appeared at Colonial Cottage in his rattley

Studebaker. He came for Kirsten, who welcomed him with icy formality. Recognizing that his evening should not be wasted in her direction, he single-handedly transported most of the Colonial Cottage girls down to the Stables.

The Clam Bake Area was fragrant with beach plum blossoms and the cool ocean air. Everyone on the staff seemed to have arrived simultaneously and the area was bustling with activity. The electricity of early summer filled the air. Cases and cases of beer came out of nowhere and Blood Sweat and Tears kicked the party off to a solid beat. My adrenaline was pumping. I felt giddy.

I found myself wedged, quite comfortably, into a booth with Mandy, Robert and Kirsten (who had decided to come at the last minute anyway), a wiry youth called Stretch and Geoffrey, a young fry-cook.

Geoffrey had intrigued me when I met him in the kitchen earlier in the week. That evening I noticed him the moment he walked in. Few men can wear blue and white paisley slacks and get away with it. But Geoffrey could! He had conservative good looks, was quiet and self-assured and maintained an unnerving direct eye contact that began to hypnotize me. He conversed readily and intelligently on a wide range of topics. He had a quick wit and a talent for drawing everyone into the conversation.

Small talk commenced.

Arriving in a new place with new people was a heady experience for me. I could re-invent myself and become anyone I chose. My identity often took on new, magical, and sometimes fictitious dimensions. I had two particular fantasy favorites.

The first was that I had attended Northfield School for Girls. I had yearned to go there when I was younger and I had learned the fantasy so well that I could have walked the campus with my eyes closed. The alumnae office at Northfield had me on their mailing list and after a few well placed financial contributions, I was being invited to their class reunions.

My second fantasy was that I had attended Cornell Hotel School, a very prestigious possibility in the world of hotels and resorts. I had actually been accepted there, but I never sent in my deposit. I don't recall whether it was lack of funds, lack of initiative or the fact that an old boyfriend's father taught there.

Unsuspecting, I launched into my 1969 identity and Northfield and Cornell became my alma maters. Across the table from me Geoffrey took notice.

"Small world!" He sipped his beer. "So did I!"

My sip of beer became an instant gulp. I thought–I hoped–he was talking to someone else. But he wasn't. He had really and truly gone to Cornell Hotel School and had studied under my old boyfriend's father. As my luck would have it, Geoffrey had also attended Mount Hermon, the brother school to Northfield School for Girls. A double whammy! I should have known better and let the subject drop right then and there, but Geoffrey had me mesmerized. The fact that he was a few years younger than I, would have meant that our paths would not have crossed and our friends would never have known one another. The illusion still might work. I let it hang precariously in the air.

The discussion ranged from the weather (which was sheer perfection and therefore boring), to what had brought each of us to the Wentworth, to critiques of the management, to the rumored arrival of Leanne. Leanne was a juicy topic! Her legend preceded her and I envisioned a 7-foot Amazon with flowing blond tresses and an insatiable appetite for male attention. I listened to the Leanne Legends, but even my wildest imagination could not have prepared me for her arrival.

Geoffrey had me bore-sighted. Perhaps he suspected my alma mater ruse. Perhaps the beer was making my thoughts soar. Or perhaps, just perhaps, there was some real chemistry happening in that booth at the Stables.

The chemistry, if that was what it was, was most certainly not happening between Robert and Kirsten. Robert had watered down Kirsten's beer and in anticipation of her wrath had wisely headed for the Men's Room. So did Geoffrey.

I leaned against the ancient wooden stall, listening to a group trying to sing along ". . spinning wheel, got to go round . . " I was smiling inside–what a wonderful night. The old boards had generations of initials carved in the walls of the stall and the tabletop. I focused on a rustic heart and realized that it's hazy outline was not so much because of its age, but because I was just a little bit drunk.

I needed some air. Kirsten had left Robert in the Men's Room and bodily snatched young Stretch from the booth heading for the door. I didn't wait to see what Robert would do next. I slid out of the stall and followed Kirsten and Stretch outside.

The night was crisp and clear and full of undercurrents. I wandered around the Clam Bake area, breathing deeply and trying to convince myself that I was walking a straight line. The lobster cookers were huge metal caverns set back from the rocky beach. Stacks of picnic tables were piled under winter tarps, waiting to be taken out of storage. The moon was playing hide and seek behind the clouds and the glimmer it sent down revealed an ancient foundation overgrown with wild roses and vines. I pushed aside a viney mass with my foot and exposed the outer edge of what must have been a porch inlaid with elaborate ceramic tiles. I made a mental note to ask Mandy about the foundation.

I stepped over the rocky wall that separated the Clam Bake Area from the beach and found myself standing on someone's blanket. A surprised couple rolled out of an embrace and looked up at me. I waved an apology as I retreated to the other side of the wall.

What a perfect summer to fall in love. Not the forever-and-ever-till-death-do-us-part kind of love, but the kind that sends your heart soaring with magic and fireworks and lasts for as long as you let it.

I heard someone behind me and turned to find Geoffrey offering to share his beer. Beer was the last thing I wanted or needed, but I welcomed Geoffrey's company. He took my elbow and steered me towards an overlook I hadn't seen before. The clouds had parted, the moon was shining bright and stars had added their brilliance. The whole scene reflected back in rippled distortions created by the currents of the harbor. I felt Geoffrey's hands on my waist. Our fingers wove together and fireworks seemed to explode out of nowhere. He didn't have to envelop me—although he did. He didn't have to kiss me—his kiss was in his fingertips—and I was returning it.

There IS magic in first times!

CHAPTER 4

Geoffrey: The Beginning

When I returned to Colonial Cottage, Mandy peered at me over her book.

"So, do tell all!" she demanded with a voyeuristic smirk.

"Nothing to tell " I apologized.

But she knew better and so did I. My summer had begun on a delicious note. I fell into bed all warm and huggy inside . . still a little drunk but very very happy.

I knew it was dawn, and I knew I was going to have to get up, but I kept my eyes tightly shut. I had a throbbing headache and the prospect of seeing Geoffrey in the light of day was one I wasn't certain I was up to. I had no delusions that he would look as good as he had felt the night before, but I kept hoping.

An ice-cold shower set me in motion and a few aspirin took the edge off. By the time Mandy and I hit the path through the Pine Woods I was beginning to feel like myself.

I didn't have to wait long to scrutinize my fantasy of the night before.

Geoffrey was waiting inside The Zoo door. He was smiling shyly and actually–glowing! I didn't know what I ate; I didn't know where I sat; I didn't know where Mandy ended up. I was drowning in Geoffrey's eyes. We made a date to meet after work that night.

In the Main Dining Room, Mrs. Hackney, a grandmotherly florist, wheeled in a cart of fresh flowers from the Conservatory, the on-premises florist shop. Once the arrangements were on the tables the full ambiance of the Main Dining Room was revealed and it was breathtaking.

During the weeks before the Social Season began, Wentworth-By-The-Sea hosted several conventions and conferences. Members of the incoming group were firemen from all over New England. During the day every manner of fire and emergency vehicle rolled across the drawbridge and the parking lot became a rainbow of red and yellow hook-and-ladders, pumpers, foam units and ambulances. Even a few antique specials.

Lunch that day was our first opportunity to step into our roles for the summer. We donned our salmon-pink, zipper-front uniforms. The firemen were considered to be a fairly tame group. Other more raucous groups would require the pink uniforms with a gazillion buttons down the front. Those zippers were just too much temptation to other, more randy groups, but the firemen could be expected to behave.

Lunch was easy consisting mostly of cold platters from Fletch's pantry. I garnished everything properly, served coffee after the meal and felt I had done a good job. After lunch I returned to Colonial Cottage. Zack and Leslie, the 1968 Couple of The Year, had a snazzy green Thunderbird and it was backed up to the porch. It appeared that Leslie was moving into Colonial Cottage lock, stock and barrel. Un-aware of Leslie's departure from their cozy love-nest, Zack was off with his buddies at the Ski Shack. Leslie and her friend Patty-Jane were having a graphic discussion of just how tasteless life with Zack had been. Patty-Jane had the rest of Leslie's worldly goods in the back of her VW. Colonial Cottage was filling up fast!

I needed a nap and I needed NOT to think. Soon the cottage was still. Babs, Patty-Jane and Leslie had gone shopping. Mandy was at the beach. The house seemed deserted–and that is exactly what Zack and his friend, Wright, thought when they climbed through my window that afternoon as I drifted in and out of slumberland.

Zack was after Leslie's car keys. While Zack searched Leslie's room across the hall, Wright stood guard, totally unaware that I was curled under a quilt not three feet from him. I slowly opened my eyes and found myself gazing at the incredibly handsome face of Prince Charming. I was spellbound. I didn't move a muscle. I just savored the view!

Zack returned dangling his prize from his forefinger and they exited via the window from whence they had come without ever noticing me.

I made a mental note of the incident and drifted off to sleep again.

This time I awoke to Leslie's banshee scream as she discovered that Zack had been there. I wondered if Zack knew what a foolish thing he had done. Not only would he be contending with Leslie's wrath but the added venom of Babs and Patty-Jane who were close on her heels. He didn't stand a chance! I envisioned the three girls returning from the Ski Shack with Zack's scalp on a tall pole. But what of his accomplice? It seemed to me that no one needed to know about his part in the heist. Why bring down the troops on such a delightful part of the Wentworth landscape?

I looked for Geoffrey in The Zoo at dinner, but he had already eaten and was helping set up a buffet table for the Firemen's Convention. We had very little to do when there was a buffet except fill water glasses, clear empty plates, pour coffee and look attentive without hovering. Several times I caught fleeting glimpses of Geoffrey as he replenished the silver chafing dishes. The suspense and anticipation of meeting him after work made the meal drag. My tables finished and I reset them quickly but carefully. I knew the hostesses would check every station after we left.

I had agreed to meet Geoffrey at Colonial Cottage, so there was no reason to hang around until he finished. I darted through the Pine Woods and spun into the shower. No matter how uneventful a meal seemed to be, there was a kitchen smell that seemed to permeate every pore of my body–especially my hair! I washed and dried my hair, carefully styled it, then put my head between my knees and messed it up so it wouldn't look like I'd spent too much time primping. At least it didn't smell like the kitchen.

The other girls were returning from dinner as Geoffrey's shiny blue MG Midget hummed into the driveway. A sports car, of course! It fit him! Anyone who could wear those blue paisley slacks would undoubtedly drive a sports car.

It was a balmy night and we took a moment to put the top down. Geoffrey had a roster of options for the evening, but I was unable to make a decision, so we drove down the coastline through Rye. The Isles of Shoals were tiny dots on the horizon. Huge pre-historic boulders joined the land to the sea, and tidal pools between them filled and emptied as the waves broke over the rocks.

Geoffrey parked the MG and we hopped from boulder to boulder until we found a good sitting rock. We began talking about our families, our schools, our favorite ice cream flavors and we speculated on the imminent arrival of the legendary Leanne.

"She's probably going to be your roommate" Geoffrey grinned.

I had figured that third bed would be occupied at some point, but I hadn't thought it would be Leanne.

Our conversation continued like a well-choreographed dance–he'd lead, and then I'd lead. Our familiarity was very comfortable. We discovered that we had both been brought up on Winnie the Pooh and Geoffrey considered his childhood copy to be one of his most prized possessions.

The wind turned. I shivered. Geoffrey took off his jacket and draped it around my shoulders, but the rocks were becoming cold and damp. Geoffrey stood up and offered me his hand. We walked back to the car hand in hand. I liked the feel of my hand in his! Together we put the car top up, although I had been looking forward to feeling the wind in my hair.

We got in the car and tried to decide on a destination. I didn't want to go to Portsmouth, or dancing at Ladd's, or to the perpetual party at the Ski Shack. An ice cream cone seemed like an okay idea, but what I really wanted was for Geoffrey to kiss me. And he did! Fireworks and magic all over again!!! Only bigger and better and more brilliant. This time I wasn't just watching–I was part of the display!

The car didn't move all night. Now remember, this was an MG Midget. For the uninformed, an MG Midget is very very small. My head was on Geoffrey's shoulder when I woke up. My legs were folded awkwardly under me and my neck was stiff. I knew I had pixie dust in my eyes and my breath was probably awful. I wished I had some Sen-Sen. But more importantly, I wished there was a Ladies' Room nearby. I pushed the door open, extracted myself from the car and hobbled up over the nearest boulder. Relief!!! But as I was re-adjusting myself a terrific ruckus went up just to my left. It was feeding time in the duck pond of a motel not 50 feet from me. I prayed that no one in the motel had happened to be gazing out the window in the direction of my rock.

The chorus of ducks had wakened Geoffrey. He was standing by the car looking fresh and alive. Even his breath was fresh. The best I could do was to chew on a limp sprig of parsley in my jacket pocket. My mother had always told me it was nature's breath freshener.

It would have been nice to go for coffee, but we were already pushing the clock to its limits. We would have to settle for Zoo coffee.

I opened the window and leaned my head into the wind as we headed back to the Wentworth. Everything was perfect. Where I was, who I was with, and most especially who I was at that particular moment!

CHAPTER 5

Chinese Food

They say you can't judge a book by its cover, but can you tell something about a person simply from their luggage?

After lunch–another buffet, and very sumptuous–Mandy and I arrived back at Colonial Cottage to find a perfectly matched set of imitation leopard skin luggage sitting on the porch. Leanne had arrived! But where was she?

Word spread quickly that Leanne had headed immediately for Ladd's to check out the landscape. She had her priorities! I found myself silently hoping that Geoffrey had NOT gone to Ladd's.

Then, even as the thought entered my consciousness, I chided myself for worrying about whether Geoffrey might become game for this female predator. What was becoming of my carefree summer?

This awareness brought another specter out of the shadows–Glenn! Two years earlier Glenn and I had been a very intense item while I took an 18-month hiatus from college and worked in Boston. He was a very good person and very good for me. Our relationship was focused and very structured. His dream had been to build a white picket fence around me and begin to raise a flock of children. When I insisted that I complete college first, his response was that women truly did not need a college experience. It was then and there that I knew that we were not cut from the same cloth, and our intensity quickly dwindled. I returned to college and Glenn became very bitter. But still he seemed to hold out hope that once I had gotten this "college thing" out of my system, I'd be willing to ride off into the Ohio sunset with him. We had never made a clean break—it was still unfinished business. And now there was this Geoffrey person breathing excitement into my life. I felt a gnawing guilt!

I didn't have time to dwell on my misplaced loyalties. Leanne was back and ready to move in. Our new roommate! Leanne was a solidly built girl who dressed to show off all of her assets. She had naturally white-blond hair, a rosy complexion, big blue eyes, and a most dramatic cleavage. I was prepared to dislike her on sight, but to my surprise, I found her broad smile and warm manner very likable. She had a flare for the dramatic and a unique way of putting things.

Leanne's tour of Ladd's that afternoon had given her an overview of the males in the immediate area. One in particular struck her fancy. When Babs pointed out that most of the bartenders were gay (and he was a bartender), Leanne did not seem to think that obstacle was noteworthy. She continued to expound on his cute buns.

Then, as if stepping on stage, Leanne raised her fist to the sky (she must have gotten the idea from "Gone With The Wind") and swore a sacred oath:

"Wright will know who I am before the summer is over!"

Yes, the same beautiful Wright who had stepped across my windowsill. I wondered if he had the slightest idea of what he was in for. He had been targeted!

I ate dinner across from Geoffrey, and we talked about how odd it was to have approached that Stables party with the intention of just having a few beers, and here we were brushing fingertips and floating on a gossamer innocence that had not been part of the plan. He made apologies for himself for that evening, saying he had promised to visit his mother. I wondered if he had a mother. But I was just as happy to get to bed early in a proper bed.

So Geoffrey went to see Mother, and I propped my bare feet up on the porch railing of Colonial Cottage. The stars are spectacular along the seacoast!

The screen door slammed as Patty-Jane and Leslie tumbled out the door headed for Chinese food. I jumped at their unspoken invitation and the three of us packed into Leslie's T-Bird. But what about Babs? She was close behind stuffing the hot pink flounces of her nighty up under her trench coat, and we were off!

We headed for Kittery where the Dragon Seed flashed a neon welcome. Babs' attire precluded our asking for a table, so we opted for take out. Leslie and I were elected to gather up the take-out order. Neat little white boxes stacked one on the other in a brown paper bag. It smelled delicious!!! We emerged to hear Babs verbally assaulting a carload of boys who had practically rammed the Thunderbird. Babs had a customized vocabulary for such occasions!

Still gesturing, Babs stepped out of the car to let me in and yards of luminous pink ruffles cascaded from beneath her coat. There were hoots and hollers from the other car.

Leslie burned rubber as we careened out of the parking lot with the boys close behind. Leslie led them on a merry chase past the guard-house at the Portsmouth Naval Shipyard, across the Portsmouth draw-bridge and through Market Square. She knew every one-way street, convenient alley and hairpin turn in town, but still the boys kept up.

We were approaching a bumpy stretch of rural straight-away when Leslie announced "Okay, girls, we're going to loose them! Watch!"

We held our breath!

Up and over; up and over; up and over . . then in an instant she killed her lights and swung into the woods.

We watched the approaching headlights.

Up and over; up and over; up and over . . and off down the road, gone forever!

Back at Colonial Cottage I munched on a sparerib and made a mental note never to ride with Leslie again.

CHAPTER 6

June Wedding

Conventions and pre-season guests kept the resort full and bustling all through the month of June, and everyone knows that June is also the month of weddings! Wedding receptions could be held in the Ballroom or in The Ship, and couples could exchange vows in the gardens or in the gazebo overlooking the harbor. Wentworth-By-The-Sea was an idyllic setting for weddings, and I was very excited when I was asked to work one of the weddings in The Ship.

Sandy Smith, the owners' daughter-in-law, was in charge. She was a master craftsman of organization and attention to detail. She planned every place card, every napkin fold and every garnish with the bride and her family. Months of preparation, and I dare say, a small fortune had been committed to this particular afternoon wedding reception.

A crew had set up the tables according to Sandy's specifications–the head table located precisely where it should be and each guest table positioned for easy access to the dance floor. Arriving early that morning, our first task was to lay the linens and tack skirts on the serving tables. Small bunches of ivy and miniature roses secured yards of draped white damask. The bride had selected maroon napkins, which we folded into perky little castles on each service plate. Every plate, fork and piece of stemware was checked for spots. Each piece was laid out according to Sandy's diagrams. The florist arrived with a vanload of elaborate Victorian centerpieces created from dark red roses, baby's breath and globe amaranth. As each centerpiece was placed on the tables we were instructed to strew fresh rose petals aesthetically around the centerpieces. The bride was rumored to have wanted strewn herbs and petals on the floor so her guests would smell their fragrance as they crushed them underfoot, but Sandy had nixed that idea in deference to the carpet.

I felt like part of the production crew for a Broadway show waiting for opening night. The excitement, anticipation and tension were building. Those of us who were working the event jogged back to Colonial Cottage and changed into our black skirt/white blouse uniforms. I had just enough time for a quick shower and a cup of soup in the Zoo before reporting for duty at The Ship.

More flowers had arrived–cascades of roses on pedestals surrounded the head table and the dance floor and a pair of four-foot topiaries flanked the door. Bob Seixas's orchestra was warming up. The mother of the bride, with her hair perfectly coiffed, had come by for a final inspection and Sandy was graciously reviewing each detail with her. Meanwhile, in back of the Ship at a service entrance, a panel truck unloaded everything needed for the wedding (all of which had been prepared in the main kitchens of the hotel). We immediately began assembling relish trays and roll baskets along with little crystal bowls of butter curls on ice for each table. A dolphin ice sculpture was positioned on a table near the bar surrounded by a lavish cheese board and a mountain of pink shrimp.

Sandy assigned us our tables and we began to pour water, garnishing each water glass with a twist of lemon. Next, we placed fruit cups in tall goblets crowned with an orb of sorbet and a fresh mint sprig on each service plate, being careful not to disturb the napkin castles.

Just before the guests arrived, each of us was given a small rose corsage to wear to coordinate with the centerpieces. The clink of stemware mingled with dignified conversation and soft background music as we stood at attention on our stations.

A drum roll announced the arrival of the Bridal Party. Eight bridesmaids emerged from two limousines, each in a hooded maroon velvet cape. They assembled in the garden to await the bride looking very much like a line-up of Druids. A white Rolls Royce crossed the draw-bridge and slowly made it's way to the entrance. The groom, in white tails, stepped out to offer his hand to his new bride. She wore a white velvet cape that matched her maids but she had pushed back her hood to reveal raven hair, flashing eyes and a smile that would make any orthodontist proud.

A photographer appeared out of nowhere with little ladders, white reflective umbrellas and special lights. He arranged and rearranged the girls taking shot after shot of their historic day. Inside he lined them up in front of a mural for more poses as guests began to find their way to their places. Someone in the family had tucked little etched copper nametags into each napkin castle. Every guest was seated according to protocol. Finally the photographer released the bridal party and the master of ceremonies regally introduced each of them as they entered and took their places at the head table. A couple of bellmen in red weskits carried the bridal capes to the cloakroom. A clergyman offered a blessing and everyone was seated.

This was our cue to swing into action. It would not be very long before the fruit cups were ready to be cleared and steaming lobster bisques were presented to each guest. We worked in teams, moving swiftly, quietly and unobtrusively between the tables. Unlike life in the Main Dining Room, this was not an opportunity to interact with the guests. Sandy Smith moved here and there checking and rechecking details. She found someone who was allergic to lobster and sent to the main kitchen for a substitute soup. A child overturned a water glass and Sandy summoned a bus boy to mop it up. The bride whispered a request in Sandy's ear and Sandy moved deftly to the bar to request that the groom's father be served watered down drinks. We cleared the bisque cups, and crumbed the tables with little silver handled brushes. The main course was Roasted Cornish Game Hen with wild rice and mushroom stuffing. Bundles of new asparagus tied with pimento "bows" surrounded the little birds. I could tell this was not going to be a hit with the children! And sure enough, Sandy had already sent to the kitchen for hamburgers and fries. Fancy hamburgers, of course, with little flags stuck in the buns.

Cornish Game Hen takes awhile to eat and I observed that many of the society ladies were merely picking at the meal politely. I made a mental note never to order Cornish Game Hen at any wedding of mine! Asparagus is not a universal favorite either, although it looked striking. Someone clinked on a wine glass demanding that the bridal couple kiss. This ritual constantly interrupts most wedding meals. I felt sorry for the bride and hoped she had grabbed a bite to eat before the ceremony. I was sure they had had champagne in the limousine, but a quick stop at a drive-thru hamburger joint would have been a good idea.

Sandy gave the nod to clear the partially eaten meals and we once again crumbed the tables. As we cleared, the bride and groom stepped up to the cake table. The bride's gown, which had previously been concealed under the velvet cape, was encrusted with pearls and sequins and adorned with tucks and folds and a dangerously low scoop neck. She bent to cut the cake and one of the bus boys froze in mid-air, completely mesmerized by the view. Sandy gave him a quick poke.

The cake itself had been designed and created in the bakery at the rear of the kitchen complex. It was an architectural masterpiece adorned with floral confections and molded marzipan doves. I wondered whether anyone ever ate doves like that. I envisioned them being carefully boxed and stored and eventually thrown out when the bridal couple discovered ants in the box on, say, their 50th wedding anniversary.

There were traditional toasts, the champagne flowed freely, and dancing began. After serving the cake, our duties were over for the moment. We gathered in the service kitchen and one of the girls took a nibble of an uneaten Cornish Game Hen just as Sandy came through the swinging doors. She was certain to hear about that later, since eating off guests' plates was a criminal offense at the Wentworth. Sandy did, however, allow us to sample pieces of the wedding cake that were asymmetrical and unfit for the guests. The cake was moist and dense, with a hint of almond flavor. Most of the weddings I had been to served cakes that were dry and flavorless, but this masterpiece was scrumptious.

We kept a keen eye on our stations, cleared the cake plates and everything else, leaving only water and wine goblets, ashtrays and centerpieces. The remainder of the cake was wheeled into the service kitchen and we swung into action, putting each piece into a tiny white box embossed with the couple's monogram. We then piled these boxes near the door so the guests could take some cake home "to dream on".

As some of the guests wandered onto the pier to chat and have a smoke, others glided around the dance floor. This concluded our duties for the day. The bus boys would finish clearing the tables, and the bartenders would be on duty late into the evening.

It was time to return to the Main Dining Room. With the orchestra in the distance and a seagull gliding overhead, I walked past roses twined over an arbor in the garden. Perfection!

CHAPTER 7

Convention Season

June is a month of contrast. The sea and sky almost merge in a steely color. The few foggy days are almost cozy. Conventions came and went. I became adept at carrying a tray and my biceps toned up. Most of the conventioneers had a lobster and clam bake by the shore at least once during their stay. It was always a big hit! The Clam Bake area was set up with pink and white striped tents to ward off fog or misty rain, but the weather was not kind to the Grocers of Greater Boston. Their lobster and clam bake had to be served in the Main Dining Room due to a full-force northeast gale whipping up the water in the harbor. Heretofore, I had not had to carry lobsters on a tray. Lobsters are an odd and awkward shape and the plates they are put on are round. The plate-covers are also round. This becomes a balancing challenge. I managed four lobster dinners at a time during that noonday meal and I thought I was doing well. Then, just as I arrived at my station, a cruet of melted lobster butter poured over the edge of my tray onto my shoulder. It soaked into my uniform and caked in my hair. We were trained to never miss a beat and I simply moved forward with an elegant presentation of each rusty red lobster and all their accompaniments.

After the meal I realized that my uniform was not going to come clean in an ordinary washing cycle. The ladies in the Valet Shop were going to have to give me some advice. Their cubbyhole was always cozy with the hum of sewing machines, conversation and low background music. With the gale going on outside, this was a perfect place to spend the afternoon. The ladies of the Valet Shop were being craftsy. Within their realm was a vat of cast off buttons. From these they were creating lapel pins backed up with sturdy nametags left behind by conventioneers. They handed me "Ron Young, YMCA" and I began to cover his identity with layers of pink and white buttons. My masterpiece would become a Christmas gift for my grandmother. While we worked they suggested I make a paste of Axion or Biz and apply it to the butter spill just before washing the uniform. The formula had been working season after season and I was certainly not the first waitress to wear butter. Clutching my artistic creation and a sample container of Axion, I braced myself against the wind and headed for the laundry room.

Besides becoming comfortable with the routine and my surroundings, I was falling in step with Geoffrey. One afternoon we prowled through an antique shop that was off the beaten path. Geoffrey had an eye for quality and taught me how to ping crystal and look for the markings on the back of china. He told me about the Lamberton Scammell China Company, commissioned to produce individual china patterns for the big hotels, railroads and steamship companies. That evening in the Main Dining Room I carefully turned over one of the old sugar bowls and, sure enough, there it was: "Lamberton Scammell". It must have been specially commissioned for Wentworth-By-The-Sea. I memorized the pattern–moss green vines supporting random bunches of salmon and rust-colored carnations, interspersed with tiny blue forget-me-nots.

It was becoming apparent that Geoffrey and I were being viewed as an "item". Waiters, bus boys, other chefs and even some of the front office gents were warmly friendly to me, but no one asked me to go anywhere. On the other hand, the women of the Wentworth did not seem to have the same aversion to Geoffrey. Perhaps it was the MG, perhaps the paisley pants, but more likely it was his wit and charm. Geoffrey had a way of listening to people and making them feel that they mattered. He was often asked to carve the steamship roast at buffets because he was able to converse with and charm the old ladies. He was a subtle asset to management. Waitresses waiting to pick up entrees at his station in the kitchen enjoyed sparring with him. Mandy reported to me that many of them were far more blatant in their overtures towards him than I was seeing.

One evening Geoffrey and I joined the crowd gathering at Ladd's to dance and drink. Leanne was on the prowl and dressed to attract. Her sideshow was worth the price of admission. I had just discovered White Russians and was feeling very warm and delicious. Girls kept urging Geoffrey to the dance floor, but he was totally absorbed in me. How wonderful, I thought, how simply wonderful! Finally he asked me to dance and we fell into each other's arms as the DJ played "You made me so very happy...I'm so glad you came into my life." Geoffrey breathed the words into my ear as we moved together to the music.

A couple of days later Geoffrey asked me to find a suitable date for his best friend Jackson who was coming for a visit, so Mandy and I put our heads together. She would have been more than happy to go out with Jackson herself, but we concocted an even better scheme. One of the waitresses paying especially close attention to Geoffrey was Tanya, a lovely, cultured girl with silver blond hair. Mandy had made note of the fact that when I wasn't around, she was able to maneuver herself into positions that allowed her a full body press upon the unsuspecting Geoffrey. Tanya needed taming. We decided that if we fixed her up with Jackson she might turn her body presses in his direction. She might also get the wake-up call that Geoffrey was "taken".

That concept caught in my throat. If Geoffrey was "taken", then so was I. I wasn't sure I was ready for that. Yet, I couldn't imagine anyone I would rather spend my off-hours with, and I hoped he felt the same. The bottom line of this realization was that I was going to have to resolve the Glenn situation. I began the dreaded letter, mustering compassion, intuitive choices of words and anything I could recall from Psych 101. Twice I put my pen down and looked to the phone. Once I considered flying to Ohio to see Glenn face to face. Yet my pen continued to move across the paper and by the end of the day I had a document that effectively did what I wanted it to, it closed a chapter of my life.

CHAPTER 8

Fourth of July

The Social Season began the Fourth of July. The lobby of the resort was festooned with bunting, embellished with arrangements of red carnations and white gladioli bundled with big blue bows and miniature American flags. Every table in the Main Dining Room had similar arrangements and flags.

Place settings during The Season were more elaborate than the convention settings. We used more silverware and all this silver had to be polished. The older pieces were monogrammed with a simple "W" and the name "Wentworth-By-The-Sea" on the flip side of each handle. In more recent years Mrs. Smith had directed the ordering personnel to drop the monogramming since the silverware had become popular souvenirs "accidentally" acquired by guests. She was willing to part with the ashtrays in the lounges, but the silverware was becoming too pricey to continually replace.

Each waitress was responsible for the care and cleaning of the silverware on her station. The Silver Room was off the main kitchen where we could hand-wash all our silverware and polish it as needed. It was inexcusable to have even a minute tarnish on any fork on any table and fried eggs always left their mark. One wall of the Silver Room had a stainless steel counter embedded with a dozen miniature sinks placed under a bank of windows that welcomed the breeze off the back harbor. The windows also afforded a view of all personnel leaving by The

Zoo stairs–the lucky ones who were already done for the meal, or the ones Mary Hart had just given walking papers to.

The hotel was American Plan–all meals included. Guests were expected to eat in the Main Dining Room, but they had options of a Clam Bake at noon, luncheon at the Fairways, lobster or steak on the Avenida Terrace, a light meal in the Ship's Dolphin Lounge or a sandwich at the Round Robin Snack Shop next to the clay tennis courts. The Avenida Terrace also served sandwiches at midnight. One especially popular option with parents was the Rogues Gallery where they could send their young ones and enjoy a degree of vacation privacy. Miss Flipper and Miss Dolphin watched over the brood and prevented food fights.

Guests were assigned a table in the Main Dining Room for their stay and it was our job to get to know their tastes and their idiosyncrasies. Maitre d' Leo Ruth drilled into us that it was our job to make each and every guest feel that every time we had even the slightest interchange with that guest, they perceive that they were the most important person in our entire lives in that split-second of time. We received our tip at the end of their stay and if the individual waitress was successful in bonding with her guests, she could expect generosity in a tidy white envelope.

Many of the Fourth of July guests returned two or three times during The Season. Some arrived on the Fourth and stayed all summer. The summer-long guests were part of the life-style that was fast becoming obsolete.

It was even rumored that Mrs. Levy, who returned season after season, had brought in her very own interior decorator to make Room 202 uniquely hers. No one else ever stayed there.

Another regular always stayed in one of the Lanai Suites in the Colonial Wing. Her afghan hound had the adjoining suite and bellboys were expected to walk the long-legged creature every few hours.

A genteel woman from New York sat by a window overlooking the harbor where she had dined year after year. Her husband had passed away twenty years before, but her waitress was still expected to set a place for him, just in case he showed up.

Friday evening was the night of the Fourth itself. A menu with the

Wentworth dolphin entwined in the letter "W" listed the offerings of the evening: choices of four appetizers with Fourth of July names like Shrimp Cocktail Minutemen, Fresh Fruit Cup Betsy Ross, Iced Concord Grape Juice and Tomato Juice Stars and Stripes. There were three soups, two salads, various vegetables and potatoes–all with contrived Independence Day names and the six entrees of the evening were Poached Salmon with Egg Sauce, Martha Washington; Red Coat Lobster Newburg in Patty Shells; Old Glory Braised Vermont Turkey; Broiled Spring Chicken, Virginia Dare; Roast Prime Rib of Beef au jus, Bunker Hill; and Fried Ham and Eggs, Liberty Bell (for the denturely challenged).

There were ten desserts and assorted cheeses offered and we were encouraged to have every table look at the substantial wine list.

A pocket-sized program of events listed tennis lessons with Wadleigh Woods, lectures, bingo, putting contests, afternoon tea, bridge parties, the movie "The Prime of Miss Jean Brodie" to be shown in the Ship, dancing in the Ballroom, a floor show, a performance of the Wentworth Symphonietta, both Protestant and Catholic Sunday services held right on the property and, of course, Fireworks!

My station consisted of six tables in an area of the dining room that would be assigned to families. It was halfway from the front against the back wall. The desirable window tables were reserved for long-term guests, VIP's and an assorted few who tipped the maitre'd heavily. Seasoned waitresses who returned year after year serviced the window tables. I liked my station. It was close to the kitchen and I was good at juggling large parties with younger diners. My station had an added bonus of a weekend bus boy named Corby. Corby was a high school Adonis with big blue eyes and a ready smile. He was well spoken and personable and would be a tremendous asset in attending to my guests when I was in the kitchen. He worked on a construction crew during the week and the physique he acquired doing that was impressive–even under his white uniform. Corby held great promise for becoming the Wentworth heartthrob of the summer. I wondered how he had come to be at the Wentworth only on weekends. It was rumored that he had never been hired but worked for free just to be around the Wentworth scene. I later discovered that he was Cher's baby brother.

My first guests were seated early that evening: two ladies traveling solo and new to the Wentworth. They asked me a lot of questions about the history of the resort and I made note that I should do some research. Although, I knew that the Russo-Japanese Treaty was an historical feather-in-the-cap of the Wentworth, I really wasn't sure what it was all about.

The evening meal seemed to be over in a flash. The Red Coat Lobster Newburg was a big hit and Strawberry Shortcake, Lexington Green was the favorite dessert. I personally thought that the "Lexington Green" historical attachment to the heaping red dessert was a tad grim.

After work, a large group of staff planned to build a bonfire at the Clam Bake area beach in order to watch the fireworks displays up and down the coast. Geoffrey's friend, Jackson, showed up at the appointed time and Tanya was ready and waiting. It promised to be a fun evening!

Before we could get a respectable blaze going, a thick fog rolled in, obscuring the moon and draping a spooky heaviness over the little beach. We huddled closer to the fire. Someone called for a ghost story and a bus boy began the ever familiar "Three Fingered Lewie". The over-dramatized camp story was met with boos and hisses. Silence fell over the group, as we listened to the crackle of the driftwood fire.

Then Joseph spoke up. He was cozied under a blanket with a chambermaid to keep him warm. Joseph volunteered a piece of local history: a murder! We held our breath as he began.

"There is a beach in New Castle not far from the hotel–in fact, it could be this very beach–where Louis Wagner beached his stolen dory near dawn that March night, the very year the Wentworth was being built. The events leading up to his wintry boat ride are not for the faint of heart."

(A shiver moved through the group.)

"The story actually takes place on Smuttynose Island ten miles offshore. Mostly fishermen were living on the Isles of Shoals in those days. The only house on Smuttynose was a stark red home occupied by a group of Norwegians who had come to America to seek their fortune. Since fishing was their trade, Smuttynose seemed like a good place to begin for John and Maren, Ivan and Anethe, Karen and Matthew.

This particular March day the men had planned to take their catch to Portsmouth and return home for dinner, but rough seas prevented their return trip. The three women realized that their men would not be home that night as the sun set. This was not alarming, as it had happened before and all the neighboring islands were friendly. They had no premonition of danger.

The men had supper in Portsmouth and visited with fellow fishermen. As was a usual occurrence in the pub on the waterfront, Louis Wagner showed up to burden everyone with his hard luck tales. He was penniless, as usual. The Norwegians expounded upon their plans to buy a new boat. Everyone had heard the plans, and no one paid much attention. Wagner, however, figured that if the men were saving for a boat, the money would probably be hidden somewhere in the Smuttynose house.

A grim plan formed in Wagner's warped brain. He knew that the tide would soon turn and as it went out the current could sweep a small boat (with him in it) well out to sea before he would have to dip the oars in the water. He knew the men would not be going home that night and he hoped the women were sound sleepers. He left the pub cogitating on his idea. As luck would have it, someone had carelessly left the oars in their dory and Wagner seized his opportunity.

The current was indeed strong and the little boat was hastened along by the nasty weather. Even so, Wagner had to row many miles before he reached Smuttynose. As he rowed he cursed a splinter he had driven into his hand as he commandeered the dory. His demeanor was darkening.

As he pulled the dory onto the beach he made note of the flickering lights on nearby islands. He wanted to be very sure their owners were sound asleep before he made his move. Most especially he wanted to be sure the three Norwegian women were asleep. He moved stealthily around the island scouting to be sure no one else was there, and then he waited.

Finally, he approached the house in the dark. The women had no reason to bolt the door nor even to draw the shades. Wagner peered through the window and saw Maren and Anethe sleeping with their little dog beside them. He figured Karen must be sleeping upstairs.

Slowly he entered through the kitchen door, crossed to the bedroom door and barricaded the women inside with a strong stick. His plan was working well. He planned to find the money and be gone before anyone was disturbed.

Suddenly, the little dog began to bark. Wagner was startled. Then from behind him in the shadows he heard Karen stirring. She had apparently gone to sleep on the sofa near the warm stove that night.

Next Maren began to tug on the barricaded door, shouting to Karen and trying to waken Anethe.

Wagner turned to the half-awake Karen in the shadows and lunged at her with a chair. They struggled. Karen fell against the bedroom door, dislodging the heavy stick. She lay under the table in a stupor. Wagner still thought the other two women were barricaded in the bedroom. Just then Maren burst through the door, put her arms under Karen and dragged her backwards into the bedroom. Anethe was beginning to rouse, but was not yet awake. Maren pushed the bed against the door not knowing what would happen next. She tugged at Anethe, pushed her out the window and urged her to run for help. Anethe lowered her bare feet into the snow and started around the house. Wagner grabbed an axe from the wood box and headed out the door and around the house. He and Anethe met head on! With a single blow he crushed her skull and she slumped into the snow, dead. Wagner's darkness overcame him and he continued to hack and slash until she was a ghastly mess...and quite undeniably dead.

Wagner returned to the house for the other two women with blood on his hands. First he went after Maren. She was strong and she was awake. She needed to be silenced. Maren ran to the bedroom window as she heard Wagner enter the kitchen. She jumped into the same snow drift as Anethe had, clutching her little dog in her arms. As she jumped, the axe Wagner had used on Anethe smashed into the sill behind her breaking the handle clean in half, the axe head flying out the window. Maren blindly fled into the darkness.

Wagner now turned back for Karen who had been crumpled on

the bed, but she wasn't there. She had dragged herself back into the kitchen.

As Maren ran past the hen house she heard Karen's screams as Wagner pummeled her with the axe handle. He had to silence Karen before her screams woke the neighboring islanders. He took out his handkerchief, gagging her, and straggled her with his hands. Peering at her life-less body in the lantern light, Wagner was not content until he had hacked her up as well.

Wagner then went in search of Maren. He could not find her. A gale had blown fresh snow across her footprints leading to the eastern end of the island. At the end of the island Maren wedged herself between some rocks at the water's edge, curling around her dog for warmth. Wagner finally gave up looking. He assumed she was either frozen or drowned, but dead in either case.

He then returned to the house and began his search for the rumored money. He found a few Norwegian coins, which he scornfully threw on the floor. His bloody finger marks were left on every cabinet, drawer and closet shelf. He had rifled through the linen closet, missing the $600 savings by the simple fold of a sheet. He was frustrated and angry and tired and hungry. Before returning to his hijacked dory he made himself a sandwich. He must have been repulsed by the bloody prints his hands made on the white crusty bread, for he took time to stop and wash up.

He headed for New Castle, thinking it would be longer and harder to row back to Portsmouth. Entering New Castle harbor, he probably looked up at the Wentworth silhouette, the tower and roof construction almost complete.

Back on Smuttynose, Maren remained in her hiding place until dawn, fearful that the tide might drive her from her sanctuary. At dawn she heard the carpenters begin work on Star Island. She tried to hail them, but they did not understand. With torn and frozen feet she made her way to the breakwater leading to the adjoining island. There the family took her in.

Quickly the story pieced together. The men of the islands and some of the workmen armed themselves in case Wagner was still on the island. They searched every nook and cranny, but he was gone.

As they finished their search the Norwegian men sailed around the point. From another island they were signaled to come ashore. Confused rumors told of trouble! Matthew and John raced to the cottage where Maren was being tended to. Ivan was frantic looking for Anethe and scrambled up the snowy beach and headed for the red house. He was leaning in the doorway in a stupor when the others caught up with him. The butchered, stiff, mangled body of his dear Anethe lay before him. They found Karen equally brutalized in the kitchen.

From New Castle, Wagner made his way to Portsmouth where he boarded a train for Boston. It was there that he was apprehended and returned to Portsmouth. There was a trial, a conviction and a hanging. Justice was done!

But it is said that on a dark night the stones that mark the graves of Anethe and Karen glow.

"Check it out!" Joseph finished "Harmony Grove, Old South Cemetery on Sagamore Road." You'll definitely find them–glowing!"

CHAPTER 9

Fire At Pebble Beach

The evening of the Fourth of July had been successful. Jackson and Tanya appeared to have been compatible, sharing a six-pack of Bud and a blanket by the bonfire. Jackson sent back rave reviews of the evening and I was hoping that Tanya was equally enamored and would redirect her attention. Alas, my hopes were not to be realized.

Through the grapevine (the most efficient and wide-spread communication device of all-time), came word that Tanya had ooed and ahhed over Geoffrey's wit and charm and clever stories. This puzzled me. I knew I had been there, cuddled against Geoffrey's left shoulder, but I couldn't quite recall the context of her observations. The only comment I heard about her encounter with Jackson was that his technique for ending the evening was a "hit and run kiss". It appeared that the Tanya trouble was going to have to be re-addressed.

Meanwhile, back in the kitchens, preparations were being made for the Saturday evening theme dinner. Since the Fourth of July had fallen on a Friday, a second elaborate dinner with creative menu offerings had been planned with an international flare called Peace To All Nations: The Olive Branch Dinner.

Each Saturday throughout the Social Season, theme dinners were the highlight of the week. Decorations throughout the resort reflected the theme and special events were planned. Even the Main Dining room colors and centerpieces were changed to enhance the theme and our uniforms were embellished to complete the picture.

Social Season meals could be anything a guest wanted. We served chocolate cake for breakfast and oatmeal for dinner if a guest requested it. I had one gentleman who liked to take a long morning constitutional at dawn and would arrive at the Main Dining Room 45 minutes before the doors opened. He expected his table to be ready for him. Religiously, every morning, I prepared a small bowl of oatmeal with exactly ¼ cup of applesauce on top, sprinkled with cinnamon and crowned with 5 plump, pitted prunes. Whenever he was a guest, my days began an hour earlier than normal.

Colonial Cottage and Rock-A-Bye Trailer were at full occupancy. No one focused on the dormitory fire in April but speculations about its origin were always lurking in the background. Management did not like the "f" word: fire. Nevertheless, there were rumors that there had been a small blaze in the Ballroom during a librarian's convention...contained and hushed up. Word was that the Valet Shop had been hit by a short-lived but smoky event, and that a would-be employee lounge had been gutted by a conflagration of suspicious origin. Everyone was nervous.

Besides Colonial Cottage, another dormitory had been created just down the shore in Rye. It was a converted motel called Pebble Beach. A two-bedroom apartment over the office of the former motel became home to five female staff members with whom Geoffrey and I had become friendly. We often joined them for a swim in their pool after work.

Kirsten had moved to Pebble Beach. She always had a cold beer in the fridge and a jolly greeting. She shared a bedroom with Cory, one of the front office employees who was just a little too prim and proper. Cory never unpacked, but kept her belongings neatly stowed in a set of American Tourister suitcases under the bed.

The other bedroom was assigned to two arrivals from California. Their VW was loaded with a backseat full of stereo equipment. Even before their toothbrushes were unpacked they had sent the swaying tones of Orpheus echoing across the rocky shoreline–"Da da da da da da da–I can't find the time to tell you...."

The fifth member of the little household was Blair. She had been hired as a hostess and arrived with an extensive wardrobe of formal dresses with "Dry Clean Only" labels. She was the self-appointed House Mother of the Pebble Beach girls.

The Wednesday after the Fourth of July weekend, Kirsten and I were re-setting our stations after lunch when Mr. Ruth approached.

"There's been another fire", he whispered "at Pebble Beach".

Kirsten bolted from the Main Dining Room. A few seconds later

Geoffrey waved from the kitchen door to get my attention. I shoved my unfolded napkins into the side-station and had my apron off before I reached the kitchen door.

It was a tight squeeze in the MG Midget as we careened out of the parking lot. We could see black smoke along the coastline, and as we got closer we could see the entire superstructure engulfed in flames with fire engines blocking the road.

We abandoned the MG and sprinted the several blocks to the fire. Firemen had begun to pitchfork burning piles of clothing out the windows. As we approached, a stereo speaker hurdled from a window in a ball of flames. There wasn't much we could do until the fire had been extinguished, so Geoffrey and I left Kirsten at the fire scene and sped off towards Hampton where Geoffrey's parents lived. If we were going to help Kirsten salvage anything, the lunch-box size trunk of the MG was not going to be adequate. We needed Geoffrey's father's Pontiac.

Having never met his folks, I began to get the jitters but I didn't have time to develop a full-fledged anxiety attack. We were in his driveway in no time. He whirled into the house, and reappeared with a set of keys. We switched cars and were headed back to Pebble Beach before I realized that I STILL hadn't met his folks.

Firemen were kicking through the rubble looking for anything that glowed. Kirsten was piling clothing beside a fence, soot on her uniform and sweat on her brow. She was examining a charred piece of furniture that must have been a bureau. A small metallic jewelry case had become liquid in the heat and welded Kirsten's high school class ring to the bureau top. The top drawer was full of acrid jerseys and underwear. Hoping that the Colonial Cleaners might be able to work miracles, we backed the Pontiac up to Kirsten's pile and heaped everything we could into the trunk. I doubted whether Geoffrey's father's car would ever smell the same again. We made two runs to the cleaners. We helped Cory transport her American Touristers and discovered that most of her belongings were spared due to the technology of the suitcase manufacturer.

After the firemen left we stood back to survey the scene. The entire apartment had been reduced to blackened beams and some droopy roof sections. The outside staircase was still standing and at the head of the stairs a lone pink waitress uniform, hung out to dry, swayed in the breeze.

James and Margaret Smith were the hotel owners. As traumatic as this fire had been for the Pebble Beach girls, the Smiths felt the loss just as sharply. Not only had they lost tangible property but also the services of five employees who were wandering around helpless and confused. Getting the girls comfortable and grounded was important both charitably and as a business decision.

All five were transported to the massive Rockingham Hotel in downtown Portsmouth, also owned by the Smiths. The ancient brick building was old, dark and needed updating, but it seemed to be a perfect solution for the employee housing crunch. Each girl was given a stipend of cash to pick up new underwear, makeup and a few clothes. Mary Hart opened the doors of the Personnel Office to assist the girls in filing insurance paperwork and lending an ear to their tales of woe.

Despite the efforts of management to return the lives of the five victims to a state of normalcy, the two California girls were already packing their now sooty VW and were headed south by sundown, but Kirsten, Cory and Blair seemed to have adjusted well–or were so spaced out and tired that they just didn't care anymore. I felt hot, sticky and smoky, and desperately needed a shower, after which, I barely had time to blow dry my hair before dinner.

Spareribs were always a messy meal, so after the feast we had to provide fingerbowls filled with warm water and heated towels. After dinner I re-set my tables, changed into my civilian clothes and collapsed into Geoffrey's father's car to wait for him. I found a Wet-Nap in the pocket of my uniform and wiped its cool lemon contents over my sweaty brow and down my neck. It was heavenly! I must have dozed off, for Geoffrey's hand on my shoulder startled me. He gave me a playful half-hug and nuzzled my neck. He commented on my lemonness and I was pleased that I had thought to use the Wet-Nap. I made a mental note to carry them with me at all times and look into the fruity freshness of Jean Nate.

We headed for Hampton to return the Pontiac and as we drove, Geoffrey talked about what had brought him to the Wentworth. He was on a quest. He had youth and time on his side and he had developed a plan to accumulate all the practical knowledge he possibly could at the tutelage of various types of employers. He intended to mold this information into a working database that he would use to open his own restaurant someday. His stint at the Wentworth satisfied his requirement for exposure to a large resort with a sizeable kitchen crew, working as a team to bring about the end result that satiated the palates of the discerning clientele.

The next step in his plan would involve "doing the circuit"–working at a northern resort in the summer and southern climes in the winter.

He paused in the description of his plan to run the Pontiac through a car wash. The strain of the day was catching up with us and silliness had raised her unpredictable head. The car had a smoked glass moon roof, and as it was pulled forward by the car wash cogs, Geoffrey and I pressed our faces against the moon roof as the big soapy brushes churned overhead. We squealed at the sensation.

Breathless from laughing, we pulled up beside the MG. Geoffrey's mother had cookies for us and gushed warmth and enthusiasm over Geoffrey's new friend: me! Whatever he had told the home front about me must have been glowing, because I was nearly smothered by the welcome.

Our visit was short but demonstrative. I liked his Mom and there was no doubt in my mind that she LOVED me. I wondered what his previous ladies had been like.

As we wound along the shore in Rye, I was overcome by the feeling of how honored I was to be his lady of the hour! I snuggled my head into his shoulder catching a lavender whiff of aftershave. Then I slept.

CHAPTER 10

Lobster and Clam Bakes

Geoffrey and I requested a day off together in mid-July. The day I walked into Mary Hart's office to fill out the request form, I felt like I was making some earth-shaking commitment akin to filing for a marriage license. I hadn't planned on allowing my life to revolve around Geoffrey, and yet it was happening…very naturally.

We decided to drive to Amesbury, Massachusetts where Geoffrey had grown up. His friend, Jackson (the "hit and run" kisser) lived with his parents on a point of land jutting into the river where we planned to have a lavish lobster feed. For this event Jackson had opted to find his own date.

The afternoon was as blue as coastal days can get. There was a steady onshore breeze keeping the heat of July at bay and sweeping any daring mosquitoes off our point of land.

Geoffrey had made elaborate seafood hors d'oeurves–scallops wrapped in bacon, a clam pate and oysters on the half-shell. Jackson's date, Wendy, was squeamish about the oysters and suspicious of the clam pate, which prompted Geoffrey to classify her as unenlightened.

Geoffrey had also brought several bottles of wine. He presented a glass to each of us and I didn't dare critique it. Somehow I knew Wendy was going to do that for us. And she did!

A caldron of water boiled on the stone barbeque pit waiting for the live lobsters to plunge in for their last swim. Wendy had bonded with one of the creatures and was asking the age-old question of whether lobsters scream when they are dropped into the boiling water. Geoffrey feigned a trip to the house to use the bathroom and I saw him circle around behind the barbeque pit. As Jackson lowered the first of the lobsters into the water a piercing scream filled the air. Wendy fell back in terror as Geoffrey emerged laughing so hard he could hardly stand up.

Jackson was disgusted. The sparring between Geoffrey and Wendy intensified and our quiet afternoon lobster bake became a battle of wits for which Wendy was ill equipped.

After dark we headed back to the Wentworth and it was then that I realized just how much Geoffrey had had to drink. Fortunately, there was no traffic on the highway as I found myself steadying the wheel whenever the MG started to cross into the adjacent lane. The drive back seemed to take forever, but somehow we managed to survive the excursion.

Back in Colonial Cottage I was wondering whether the exercise of planning a joint day off had been worth it, then I recalled the look on Wendy's face as the lobster screamed and I decided it was.

Clam Bakes at Wentworth-By-The-Sea were very different. They were held every Friday at high noon and waitresses were known to wage war over the privilege of working them. At last, my turn finally came.

At dawn an enormous stainless steel cauldron was packed with lobsters, clams and corn-on-the-cob. A Clam Bake Master stood guard all morning, making sure the propane burners produced the right amount of steam to bring these delicacies to their full potential. Meanwhile, we packed the hotel panel truck with steaming vats of clam chowder, tubs of potato salad and coleslaw and wicker laundry baskets heaped with fresh-baked rolls.

For these weekly events we could wear whatever we liked and it amazed me how Leanne could look seductive even in denim coveralls.

By lunchtime all was ready. Billows of steam puffed skyward as the heavy canvas covers were drawn back to reveal the rosy pink lobsters, clams and corn still in the husks.

Hotel guests lined up to be served. A random mid-westerner would opt for chicken but most were ready to tackle the famed New England lobsters. The guests seated themselves at green picnic tables while seagulls hovered overhead looking for tidbits. We wandered among the guest tables offering beverage refills and helping novice lobster-eaters attack the hard-shelled critters.

After the guests had been made comfortable, each Clam Bake worker was offered a plump lobster with broth and butter and all the accoutrements.

We perched on flat boulders overlooking the beach and feasted. No wonder waitresses were willing to sacrifice days off to work the Clam Bakes.

Cleanup after the Clam Bakes was nothing more than policing the area for stray napkins and lobster shells. Not only did we have the chance to eat like royalty, but we had minimal work to do and a chance to bask in the sun. How much better could life get?

Later that evening Geoffrey and I wandered along the shore, picking up flat rocks and skipping them across the gentle swells. I was gleefully rubbing in the fact that I had dined on lobster two days in a row while he was slaving in the hot kitchens. Between talking and walking we came to a secluded sandy place between the salt marsh and the rocky ledges. We spread a blanket on the sand and stretched out. The tide gently lapped against the shore and the night peepers affirmed that summer was fully upon us.

We kicked off our shoes and rolled our windbreakers up as pillows. Laying on our backs the stars seemed closer than ever. A wayward sea bird out after its curfew soared by and shooting stars entertained us. Geoffrey's big toe caressed my ankle and we seemed to blend into the landscape.

I must have drifted off for I woke up with a start as an icy ripple nibbled at my bare toes. The tide had turned! Geoffrey cracked his forehead against my chin as he came to life. We scrambled to our feet to survey our fast disappearing paradise. The salt marsh was already under water. We grabbed the dampened blanket and scurried up the ledges. Laughing breathlessly we watched our beach disappear. As the last inch of sand sank below the waves we saw a pale pink windbreaker drifting out to sea.

"I'll buy you a new one!" Geoffrey whispered.

CHAPTER 11

The Prince Charles Ball

My station was always full.

One week a couple of darling little grandmothers entertained their grandchildren. I thoroughly enjoyed the bustling family and looked forward to their arrival at mealtimes. The children took their evening meal in the Rogues Gallery with other youngsters, but they were surprisingly well behaved and conversational during breakfast and lunch.

The family had been under my care for almost a week by the time the West Indies weekend began. To the delight of my young guests the busboys and waiters dressed as pirates, wearing eye patches and billowy white shirts opened enough to reveal buccaneer chests. Young Tara almost swooned when she was introduced to my weekend busboy, Corby. She had been politely bored most of the week and Corby added a new dimension to her vacation. Unfortunately, Leo Ruth was chatting with the grandmothers when the mutual Corby/Tara attraction became apparent. Corby was summoned and endured a "fatherly talk" in a corner of the kitchen. He returned to my station stiff, efficient and silent. The maitre'd had made it abundantly clear that there was to be very limited interchange between staff members and guests. Corby was encouraged to be polite and helpful. A little flirting was allowed, but beyond that he was merely attractive scenery for the guests' daughters. He was ordered not to get any closer. Those were his facts of life!

The facts of life at Wentworth-By-The-Sea had a definite socio-economic bias. There was a not so subtle cast system that had been in place for generations. A vintage brochure advertising the resort boasted, "Careful selection of clientele, restricted to ensure a congenial atmosphere."

One bright afternoon a group of apparent ruffians stepped up to the front desk announcing that they had reservations. The group was a popular band, The Association ("Cherish is the word I use to describe..."), and they had a gig at the Hampton Casino. The desk clerk was horrified in that the assumption had been made that The Association was a business group, not a band. Reluctantly the front desk honored the reservations and the front desk clerk who had made the reservation was given a rap on the wrist.

Even more telling had been an incident only a few years before when one of the conventions had scheduled a Black speaker. Management told the convention organizers that Wentworth-By-The-Sea would not allow a Negro to be part of their program. Desperate for the use of the Wentworth's facility, the convention cancelled their Black speaker. I wondered whether that could have happened in 1969.

On July 1st the international news headline had been the appointment of Prince Charles as the Duke of Wales. After the ceremonies and celebrations in the British Isles, he launched a world tour with Portsmouth, NH as one of his first stops where he would arrive on a British Naval vessel. Wentworth-By-The-Sea seemed the most appropriate place for the town fathers to entertain the future king of England. It was a most auspicious event and a formal ball was planned.

The announcement sent shivers down my spine. Prince Charles was the closest thing I could think of to a contemporary Prince Charming. (Besides the bar tender, Wright, that is!) He was regal, charming, and witty and was adored by most of the world. And he was still an eligible bachelor, despite Richard Nixon's attempts to pawn his daughter off on the young Prince. Despite opinions to the contrary, I felt that there was still a place for the Royal Family in a society that hungered for heroes. The fact that the royals lived in palaces, rode in coaches (or at the very least Rolls Royce's), kept stables of horses, traveled the world and represented the best of English culture made Prince Charles a very mystical figure. And he was coming to the Wentworth!

Her Majesty's flagship carrying Prince Charles and his entourage arrived at the Portsmouth Naval Shipyard. Shore leave for the crew was anticipated and most of the young ladies of the Wentworth wanted to rub shoulders with our British guests. Unfortunately, I had to work late and I felt that the world was passing me by.

The Ball itself had been arranged and planned by a committee of the most pedigreed Portsmouth socialites. White wicker birdcages dripping with pastel flowers reflected in the Ballroom mirrors. Young ladies from the seacoast area were carefully selected as escorts for Prince Charles' crew. The dressmakers, hair stylists and florists of Portsmouth were working 'round the clock preparing for The Prince Charles Ball. It was a scene right out of Cinderella with Prokofieff's music exuding from every doorway up and down the seacoast.

But let's get back to the anticipated shore leave. Everyone in town wanted to meet, greet and be seen with the handsome British crewmembers. Two of the Wentworth waitresses hit pay dirt when they caught the eye of two young cadets.

These two young ladies were full of spunk and their thirst for adventure had brought them up from Georgia to experience New England. They were vicarious beauties with style, charm and sparkle. One couldn't blame the crew members for noticing them across a crowded room.

The girls and their new British friends partied way into the night until the gents had to be back on board their vessel. The well-meaning cadets eagerly invited the girls to attend the Ball with them the next evening.

At roll call the next morning the girls were beside themselves with excitement as they approached Leo Ruth with the request for the evening off. The rest of us watched with bated breath. Mr. Ruth looked at them out of the corner of his eye, shifted his massive weight onto the other foot and faced them squarely.

"No!" he stated simply.

The girls were aghast. They were willing to work someone else's shift, forfeit future days off or be docked pay. They didn't expect such a flat, immovable answer.

He continued. "You are waitresses. Waitresses don't go to the Ball."

Such a stigma to the name "waitress"! No matter what one's background was; no matter how educated or connected; no matter how charming–the label "waitress" was indelible.

The trade-off was clear: a steady, secure place to live and work for the rest of the summer or one spectacular evening of glamour. We watched them agonize over their decision for a full 30 seconds. Glamour won out!! The rest of us began to applaud and then thought better of it as the two girls handed their aprons to Mr. Ruth and went to pack their bags.

The night of the Ball we had a full house and I was busy at my station in the Main Dining Room. I never saw the limousines pull up under the port cochere–or perhaps Prince Charles arrived in a gilded coach with white chargers. I did, however, catch glimpses of the elegant gowns and handsome uniforms. It was a very special evening and I was only two rooms away from the fairy tale itself. I was honored to be there, even as a lowly waitress. We caught sight of our former waitress friends looking like princesses themselves. They had chosen wisely. And after that night we never saw them again.

CHAPTER 12

"The Eagle Has Landed"

Life at Colonial Cottage was crowded. Mandy and I had to get up at the crack of dawn in order to get to the showers before the hot water expired. Leanne wasn't home much. When she wasn't on duty in the Main Dining Room, she was on the prowl and we never knew where she laid her head at night. The amazing thing was that she never appeared tired, puffy eyed or hung over. She was always crisp and groomed and ready to tackle the world. We figured she must function on reserves that the Eveready battery folks would love to have had a patent for.

One evening the Colonial Cottage girls decided to bicycle to the ice cream stand up the road. The heat of the July night was stifling and the cool, slow melt of Peppermint Stick Crunch on my tongue was heavenly. Leanne had shooed us off for ice cream with particular vigor that evening, leaving her alone at Colonial Cottage. We all assumed she had some extra-curricular activities lined up. We speculated on who the man of the hour might be. We knew we would find out at breakfast. Each morning The Zoo became her stage as Leanne expounded on her exploits of the evening before, as we listened, wide-eyed and blushing.

Breakfast came and we chided each other on our voyeuristic anticipation of Leanne's tales. None of us had met anyone like her!! The morning after the ice cream stand soiree her story was about a "tender young thing" she had plucked from the ranks of the junior waiters.

Beau was tall, slender, a bit awkward and very quiet. Leanne's worldliness and Beau's innocence was an unnatural combination .. but nothing surprised us. Unsuspecting, Beau entered The Zoo and heard his name mentioned even before he poured his first cup of coffee. The poor fellow headed straight for Mary Hart's Office to hand in his resignation. He was mortified! But, alas, he never realized the potential of the positive publicity Leanne had afforded him. He had turned in his uniform, packed his bags and was heading into the sunset totally unaware of the number of staff members who were taking careful note of Leanne's graphic review of his prowess.

The Wentworth-By-The-Sea staff was spread out up and down the seacoast. A number of waiters lived at Pioneer Village in Rye, which was once a boys' camp. A couple of former barracks buildings by the Coast Guard station had also been leased for the summer along with an odd collection of cottages and houses around the area. Geoffrey and I were invited to one of those cottages the evening of July 20th.

All day long there had been excitement in the air. Guests clustered in the Foyer and the parlors around televisions and the topic was universal: Apollo 11 was about to land on the Moon.

We were eating supper in The Zoo when someone came in with a portable radio. A hush fell over the group. The voice of Astronaut Neil Armstrong crackled from the speaker:

"Houston. Tranquility Base here. The Eagle has landed."

The Americans in their tiny space vehicle were actually sitting in the Sea of Tranquility...on the Moon.

When I was in elementary school the first satellite had been launched. I was very young at the time, but it made enough of an impression on me that I remembered that something quite extraordinary had happened. And not ten years later we were listening to the voice of an astronaut on the Moon. What a feat to have gotten so far that fast!

The evening meal went quickly, winding down the Miami Revue weekend. It was Sunday and many guests had checked out and the newcomers were just arriving. I was preoccupied with thoughts and images of the astronauts resting and preparing for the first daring step outside the capsule. I tried to imagine their excitement–it was an excitement that captured the imagination of the entire world.

After the Main Dining Room was buttoned up and the plastic flamingos from the weekend had been packed away, I waited in Geoffrey's car. The kitchen crew always got out later than we did, but this particular evening they all wanted to get to a television as soon as possible, and Geoffrey appeared in record time.

There was no time to unwind that night. No shower, no cold beer. We buzzed off to New Castle and the cottage dorm where the biggest and best TV in the area was located.

The living room was packed. We grabbed a seat on the floor and I felt a tightness in my gut. Excitement! This was historical!! History books were going to write about July 20, 1969.

The television anchor was reviewing the backgrounds and accomplishments of the three Apollo 11 astronauts, Armstrong, Aldrin and Collins. This was followed by re-runs of the launch four days earlier and a repeat of Armstrong's historic words: "The Eagle has landed!" Close to 10:45 the signal went live to the Eagle on the surface of the Moon. The initial images were distorted and upside down. Neil Armstrong was opening the hatch. The images cleared and righted themselves. We held our breath collectively. He descended the ladder. At 10:56:20 Armstrong stepped to the surface and declared: "It's one small step for man, one giant leap for mankind."

Everyone in the room cheered. Everyone in the world cheered.

In that moment–as I sat wedged into a tiny living room in New Castle, New Hampshire–I felt that the entire world must be united in that one word: "Mankind".

In lieu of champagne, our group lifted an assortment of beers and malt beverages–toasting the first Man on the Moon.

People began to leave, but Geoffrey and I wanted to see the re-runs on the Late News. It was then that we heard the SECOND biggest story of the day.

While Apollo 11 was winging its way through the heavens there had been a mishap on Martha's Vineyard. Senator Ted Kennedy's car had plunged off a bridge at Chappaquidick Island killing his young passenger, Mary Jo Kopechne. The press was having a field day! The pride, honor and glory of the Apollo 11 landing was practically overshadowed by the speculations, innuendos, fabrications and accusations spewing over the airwaves. They say bad news makes headlines…and Chappaquidick certainly was doing that. I imagined that the name Mary Jo Kopechne would ring down the corridors of history and haunt the Kennedy family forever. How many people would know the names of the three Apollo astronauts in twenty years? The media angered me.

Geoffrey sagely observed: "Man at his best and Man at his worst!"

I sparked back with, "NO! The media at it's best and the media at it's worst!"

Driving back to Colonial Cottage we stopped to watch the stars and check out the Moon. It looked so bright and familiar–but it was different now.

CHAPTER 13

First Love

Our mail was sorted and tucked into alphabetized pigeonholes in The Zoo. Most of us picked up our mail just before lunch and spent the meal browsing letters from home and trying to ignore the bills. Geoffrey shared most of his personal correspondence with me–introducing me to the authors of letters he received with lavish vignettes about them.

It was a particularly busy week preceding the Christmas in July weekend. I had spent the morning setting up some new tables and organizing my station and I was late for lunch. I looked around The Zoo for Geoffrey and found him isolated in a corner, engrossed in his mail. We had both been suffering from exhaustion and our nerves were on edge. But I wasn't prepared for the icy reception I got. Whatever was in that letter was for his eyes only. His silence and chill were impenetrable. I sat alone, ate hastily and headed back to work.

As I maneuvered through my luncheon duties I dealt efficiently and impersonally with the kitchen staff–particularly with Geoffrey. I stayed out of his way. After lunch I stepped out the door in time to see the dust he had left behind as he careened out of the parking lot. I was puzzled, but not totally surprised. The passion with which we had fallen into each other's lives was bound to level out–or maybe even burn out. The emotions were too intense to hold up in day-to-day living. Perhaps we needed a break from one another.

Mandy was surprised to see me after lunch. I was usually off with Geoffrey most afternoons. She looked inquisitive but before I could formulate an answer to her unspoken question, Leanne chimed in. (Leanne always knew anything that was worth knowing and plenty she shouldn't have known.)

"Geoffrey is in mourning!" she laughed. "His first love is getting married!"

I was startled.

Leanne continued dramatically "You know, they say you never get over your first love. Now as for me…"

Mandy cut her short with a piercing glance.

I liked standing near my guests as they talked at dinner. I was curious about their lives and their opinions. I would position myself just within hearing range, but not close enough to be noticed. Two couples were talking about the effects of chemical fertilizers on food crops. I had a hard time getting interested in the amount of potassium found in modern bananas as opposed to bananas ten years ago. My interaction with the kitchen staff was again efficient and impersonal.

After dinner I decided to go into Portsmouth with Cher and her boyfriend. They were headed for Fisherman's Pier. I left them at the restaurant and wandered into Prescott Park. I sat on a bench facing the busy Piscataqua River and watched a couple of tugs nudge an oil tanker through the drawbridge.

I thought about what Leanne had said about first loves. She was right about some things. There was certainly something very unique and special about first love. There were no expectations, no cynicism, no fear of rejection, and no baggage, just an overwhelming sense of surprise at every new discovery.

I thought back to an earlier summer on Cape Cod and Scott. It was my first summer away and I felt a little awkward, a little homesick and a little out of place until I met Scott. And just like it is supposed to be, there were fireworks and skyrockets and shooting stars for no other reason than the fact that Scott and I walked the face of the same planet. I marveled at his sensitivity, romantic spirit and creative humor. He drank in the world and reflected it back. He reveled in the smallest wonder and, to my utter surprise, he reveled in me–in us! We walked the beaches of the Cape that summer, swam, laughed, slid down the dunes in Truro on cardboard box toboggans. We lived that summer for and in one another. But inevitably Labor Day came. I remembered "our" song: "We'll sing in the sunshine. We'll laugh every day. We'll sing in the sunshine. Then I'll be on my way."

The night before I left, Scott and I had stayed up to watch the late summer sunrise over Pleasant Bay. Basking in that sunrise of innocence and idealism we had vowed to return to that very sand dune on Labor Day four years later when we could reasonably expect to have finished college. No matter what transpired in between, we had a date that was sacred.

And Labor Day "four years hence" eventually did come. Scott never knew that I actually showed up. It was raw, foggy and damp. I spent the day sketching. I only half expected Scott to show up and when he didn't appear, I knew that I would never see him again.

I figured Scott would have made a wonderful life for himself. Although I was curious to know what had become of him, I realized that this was now a closed chapter for me.

I wondered how my heart would respond if I received a letter announcing Scott's engagement. My scars were well healed, but perhaps Geoffrey's were not. There was so much I didn't know about Geoffrey. And some things I probably shouldn't know.

I pulled the damp wool of my sweater tighter around my shoulders, breathed a deep sigh and smiled out loud. I was glad Geoffrey was neither my first love, nor I his. I had arrived at the summer of 1969 with a richer understanding and appreciation of life, partly because of my Scott. Geoffrey, however, still had not completely let go of his Kathy. I blew a kiss to the wind, figuring that the wind would take it to Scott, wherever he was. Then I headed back to meet Cher.

Christmas In July was upon us in no time. A life-size paper mache Santa sat in the lobby amidst a bank of artificial poinsettias. Even the influential powers at the grand old resort could not order poinsettias to bloom in July. There was a golf tournament complete with trophies, a presentation by the Rankin Marionettes and dancing in the Ballroom until midnight. Low on the list of weekend activities was a lecture entitled "Vietnam: Frontier of Frustration".

The Saturday evening Merry Christmas Dinner featured such delights as Northern Lights Poached Filet of Lemon Sole, Elfin Potatoes, and White Christmas Marshmallow Sundaes. The entire staff donned red Santa hats and sweated their way through the meal. The Wentworth Symphonietta was positioned at the front of the Main Dining Room and played Christmas carols all evening.

One of our elderly guests arrived at the Main Dining Room door in a stunning red sequin gown and asked the maitre'd to zip her up. He did so with great dignity and she proceeded to her table. As she sat down I noticed that her matching ruby red slippers were on the wrong feet. (Her nurse and companion must have had the night off.)

CHAPTER 14

Sagamore and Campbell's Island

After the Pebble Beach fire, the management at Wentworth-By-The-Sea had been trying to initiate a new master plan for housing the forty or so waitresses scattered over a ten-mile radius of the hotel. Sully, the usually jolly van driver, was beginning to look harried. It was his responsibility to get everyone to and from work. We were encouraged to leave our private cars wherever we were living, partly because it left more room for the guests in the hotel parking lot, and partly because of the unsightly nature of some of the employee vehicles. One of the waiters drove an old Plymouth decoupaged with the Sunday comic strips–every fender, every bumper. It was a unique art form that the Wentworth management preferred to have parked elsewhere. It was at this point that Sagamore raised its architecturally ugly head to provide a partial solution to their dilemma.

Sagamore was a one-story concrete-block bunker designed as a pre-school in the early 60's.

It was situated in a wooded area behind an over-crowded, poorly planned residential neighborhood located over 5 miles from the Wentworth. The pinewoods around it filtered the sunlight, and time, disuse and mildew had dulled the bright blue/orange theme that was carried from room to room. The entrance was complete with a front desk, sign-in sheet and a housemother. (Instant institutionalization!)

Mandy and I dragged our suitcases down the long hall to our assigned room. Metal lockers had been set up for our closet space and metal desks became our dressing tables. Built-ins originally planned to hold finger-paints and animal crackers became our bureaus. Four metal army cots with tidy maroon blankets had been squeezed together along one wall, side-by-side with barely a foot of clearance between them.

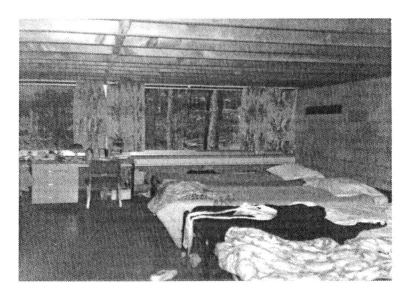

The rest of the room was spacious–almost cavernous–with its own private back door and its own private lavatory. Unfortunately the fixtures were designed for 5 year olds so we had to learn to squat.

Leanne's distinctive leopard skin luggage was already in the room and Kirsten became our fourth roommate. While unpacking, Leanne picked up one of Mandy's bras and held it up for inspection. (It looked like a training bra.) Spontaneously Leanne grabbed a magic marker and hand-printed a sign for our door: "Bitty Boobs and the Three Chests!" And that was who we became. (It was a good thing Mandy had a sense of humor.)

Moving to Sagamore from Colonial Cottage was tiring and depressing, but somehow we managed to never miss a beat between one meal and the next.

Guests came and guests went. At one point I found myself enjoying a large extended family from Massachusetts–grandparents, parents and youngsters all under the sponsorship of the great-grand-matron of the family who was guided into the Main Dining Room in a wheel chair every evening by twin 12-year-old granddaughters in starched dresses and crinolines. No one at the table lifted a fork until Gran-Marm did. Everyone waited to see what she would order and took his or her lead from her. One evening everyone ordered Prime Rib and several bottles of Chateau Haut-Brion. The children were given stemmed goblets of grape juice and toasts were made to absent or departed loved ones as well as the family members seated about the table.

At lunchtime members of my family had scattered activities going on and often the ladies of the clan were the only ones to dine in the Main Dining Room. Noontime diners were sometimes treated to chamber music or a fashion show featuring gowns and furs from Portsmouth shops, Boston furriers or the Nome Seiler Shop off the lobby. These midday meals were far more relaxed than the evening meal, and less hectic than breakfast. The ambiance gave me an opportunity to chat with my guests. They were interested in my college endeavors and even solicited my opinion on various topics over Caesar Salads and chilled strawberry soup.

After lunch I was used to checking and re-checking all the details of my station in preparation for the evening meal. Some days I was the only waitress remaining after everyone else had finished. This was never a problem when I was living at Colonial Cottage, for a brisk walk through the Pine Woods brought me to its doorstep. The Sagamore move really upset my routine and it wasn't long before I missed the van taking the Sagamore residents "home" for the afternoon. I was tired and cranky as I prepared to spend the afternoon in The Zoo reading a magazine I had bought at the News Nook. As I tried to get comfortable on a hard wooden chair, one of the broiler cooks came through The Zoo and took note of my plight. Joseph lived with his mother on the island behind the Wentworth and offered to take me with him to meet her. There I would have a chance to stretch out on a proper sofa until the evening meal. I was elated!

The road to Campbell's Island dipped inconspicuously below the clay tennis courts and traversed a causeway just above the tidal flats. There were two houses on the island. One was tall and weathered and in serious need of repair. A cluster of dirty sheep grazed around a dilapidated gazebo on a knoll behind it. The smaller house belonged to Joseph's mother. It was a tidy Dutch Colonial, solid and strong in contrast to the other house.

Joseph's mother was a short, compact lobsterman's widow who rented rooms to bus boys and provided a haven for her three grown sons whenever they were between jobs or wives. When I arrived, Kay was baking a bundt cake, lining the mold with chocolate jimmies and adding a cup of strong coffee to an ordinary store-bought yellow cake mix. I thought she was a genius! The cake rivaled anything that came out of the bakery at the back of the big Wentworth kitchens. I gratefully accepted her offer to curl up on the living room sofa, and soon I was napping.

A little while later, Joseph gently shook my shoulder. He pointed out that my pink lunchtime uniform was rumpled and even if I could iron it, the uniform for the evening meal was white. He suggested I make a hasty visit to the Valet Shop and see whether the ladies could help me out.

I slipped into my shoes and headed back across the causeway, marveling at the way the hotel took up the entire skyline from the vantage point of the island. Low heathers bordered the dusty causeway and spiky beach grass dipped and nodded in the late afternoon sun. I would make it a point to visit Kay again, and I was quite pleased to have a new friend in Joseph.

My friends at the Valet Shop found a white evening meal uniform that fit reasonably well even though it was hemmed for a midget.

CHAPTER 15

My Brother Visits Ladd's

Geoffrey had recovered from his melancholy and had been a big help during the move to Sagamore. Tanya, who was still willing to sell her soul for a little quality time with Geoffrey, was now living next door to me. She had a couple of new roommates, cousins Sil and Ally. They replaced the girls who had left at the time of the Prince Charles Ball. Sil and Ally were brazen temptresses who made a sport of being outrageous and would "accidentally" forget to wear a slip under the sheerest of uniforms. Sil wore dainty floral print panties that played hide and seek through the folds of the pink uniforms but made a definitive statement when worn under the even more transparent white uniforms. Ally also lost an eye to Geoffrey.

I was puzzled by the amount of attention Geoffrey generated. His duties as a lowly fry cook didn't exactly qualify as a position of power. Perhaps it was the car. Perhaps it was the paisley pants. I asked Mandy what she thought.

She laughed, as if the answer should have been obvious to me. He was interesting BECAUSE he was with me. It was Mandy's opinion that I could have my pick of the men at Wentworth-By-The-Sea and the fact that I displayed an obvious devotion to Geoffrey implied that he must have magic and magnetic powers that they were willing to make fools of themselves to discover. Although her theory was unique, I wasn't convinced. Neither was I convinced that Geoffrey was totally devoted to me. Tanya, Sil and Ally were all hot on his trail, but I also saw that his eye would wander towards Cher whenever her boyfriend was not around. I could tell by the way his breathing changed.

Meanwhile, Ally set up a silent rivalry with me. One afternoon I returned to discover my cot on a rocky ledge outside Sagamore with every piece of bedding and clothing laid upon it in the precise position it had been indoors. Perched on top of my cot was Ally striking an alluring pose. I saw no humor in it and my resentment towards the girl began to fester. Geoffrey sensed the steam beginning and he quickly assisted in getting my cot back to its normal resting place.

It was about this time that I received word that my brother was coming home on leave from Marine Boot Camp. He and his buddy decided to spend the weekend where the action was–with me!

I was surprised at how much resistance I encountered trying to find blind dates for the two young Marines. I was also unsure as to what military training would have done to change my brother. Finally, Katy and Sherry agreed to go out with them. Their dormitory quarters were in the big hulking Rockingham Hotel in Portsmouth. We all agreed to meet at Ladd's after work.

Geoffrey and I were first to arrive. Soon the boys came through the door looking distinctly military–clean-shaven with buzz haircuts, but quite strikingly tan and well built. The Marines had filled out my baby brother's physique admirably.

The dance floor was swaying with compacted bodies and the night air carried the lyrics to "Crystal blue persuasion". We all made ourselves comfortable and waited for the girls. While we were waiting Leanne made her nightly grand entrance. She wore a skin-tight black skirt that just barely covered her bottom and a white satin blouse buttoned a few buttons lower than most would dare. She leaned against the bar with her hand on one hip scrutinizing the dance floor as if she owned the place. Everyone knew Leanne. She had a drink in her hand in a flash and invitations to sit here and there came from all directions. All she had to decide was who she wanted.

Doug and his buddy were drooling over Leanne when Katy and Sherry showed up. They had nowhere near the visual impact of the sensuous Leanne, but a few beers later everyone was happy with their selections and Geoffrey and I could be smug about our successful matchmaking.

CHAPTER 16

Legends of Campbell's Island

The first week in August was advertised as a week of tennis activity. Lessons and demonstrations by well-known names in the tennis circuit; special attention to guests' skills by the hotel's own pro, Wadleigh Woods; competitions and tournaments and, finally, awards and trophies to be presented at the Saturday evening Tennis Ball.

The tennis matches on the terraced clay courts fascinated Geoffrey and one afternoon we found seats on a shaded bench near the lower courts from which we could watch the match in progress. I became bored and decided to take a walk across the causeway to visit Kay. I was hoping she would have an interesting tale or legend about the area to share. She had been in New Castle all her life and most certainly knew anything that was worth hearing. Kay was sitting on her back steps shelling peas when I arrived. Her eyes sparkled when I asked my question.

Kay leaned close as she began. She said that she considered herself to be a very wealthy woman. She had been married to a solid man who fathered her three sons; she had been left comfortably secure and the ocean air cleared her head every morning whether she woke to a shimmering summer morning or a blustery winter gale. The island and the ocean fed her soul. But (and she winked) she had heard tales that her island hid even more treasure than those that she had expounded.

Rumor was that a wealthy clergyman sailed to the area with the intention of using his funds to further the Lord's work. He was set upon by his shipmates, cast off on the Isles of Shoals, and his treasure buried on Kay's island. Others think that Captain Kidd left a stash somewhere in the neighborhood. There was even a treasure map. Kay had a faded copy of the alleged treasure map framed in her TV room. "For curiosity sake." she said.

She showed me the map, which depicted a bridge connecting to Blunt Island, a marking labeled "Black Point" and a sketch of a big rock with a "windowsill formation on the top". The markings indicated the treasure to be 25 rods below the bridge and 20 rods below Black Point "at low water" . . . . which brings you to the big rock. By the mapmaker's calculations there should be 3 chests of gold, a barrel of silver and a box of coins. At this point Kay laughed.

She said that long before her time, teams of treasure hunters had dredged the harbor bottom and scoured the island. Between 1880 and 1900 the quest was begun and ended over and over. Kay figured that a small fortune in dredging equipment, dowsing rods, pick axes and shovels had been spent on the obsession.

The peas were shelled, Kay's dinner was in the oven and it was time for me to go. I turned as a held open the screen door.

"Do you believe it's here?" I asked.

She winked.

CHAPTER 17

Woodstock Exodus

The previously overcrowded conditions at Colonial Cottage seemed a lot more civilized than the situation at Sagamore. The Sagamore showers were metal camp-style stalls, lined up in what had been the pre-school kitchen. The room never dried out, had no ventilator and yellow jackets were sharing residence with us.

The newly arrived waitresses took their work far less seriously than those of us who had been around all season. Sil and Ally thought nothing of killing a 6-pack between lunch and dinner and then they would rely on one of the friendly bus boys to stabilize their trays as they maneuvered from the kitchen to the Main Dining Room. Their breach of the dress codes was only part of their thumbing their noses at authority. They were perpetually late to roll call and I had watched Sil spit-shine a service plate with her apron corner instead of washing it.

Casino Royale weekend came 'round and the cousins simply didn't show up for the Saturday evening meal. What was even more amazing was that Leo Ruth didn't fire them on the spot. Perhaps he secretly enjoyed the floral panty show. Corby, the weekend busboy, was pressed into service as a waiter and covered their station. Rumor had it that the handsome young waiter received a fabulously generous tip from a group of single schoolteachers.

But Sil and Ally were not the only offenders. Discipline and precision on all fronts seemed to have become sketchy since the Sagamore move. We could come and go easily at Colonial Cottage. At Sagamore we had to work our afternoon plans around Sully's van route and often we had little or no time to relax, freshen up, re-dress and return to the Main Dining Room. To compensate for this it seemed that Sagamore was in a state of constant partying. Staff members gravitated to the old pre-school and lounged on the wide concrete windowsills laughing, socializing and drinking.

One afternoon I returned to Sagamore to find Geoffrey waiting for me with Ally straddling his lap. Six or seven bystanders watched the unsuspecting Ally who had her back to me. Geoffrey's look of terror should have given her a clue, but before she could react I grabbed her by the hair, bodily lifted her from his lap and slammed her into one of the metal lockers. She was stunned and Geoffrey's mouth dropped to the floor.

"Oh," I said to Geoffrey. "Did you want that there?"

Geoffrey muttered something unintelligible and Sil pulled her cousin out of the room and down the hall.

I sent Geoffrey home for a cold shower and gazed at myself in the mirror. How very territorial I had become! I wasn't certain I liked the image, but somehow the summer of 1969 had created some new sides to my character that I'd never seen before. I looked around and began to question my relationship with Geoffrey.

I knew that the Irish look-alike brothers had noticed me and one evening at Ladd's I had felt Chip's electrical magnetism when he rubbed his hand across my shoulders while Geoffrey was in the Men's Room. I was also aware that the sheets on his bed were considered to be one of the highest traffic zones in the realm.

Corby would have been glorious fun, but he was six years younger than I was. Disheartening scenes from "The Graduate" played in my conscience.

It would have been very pleasant to wrap myself in Joseph for a time, but we had such a delicious brother-sister thing going that I could not imagine heating that up and loosing access to his mother's cozy kitchen.

Geoffrey and I took a day off just after the Ally scene. Getting away together seemed to ground and refocus us both. We drove up into southern Maine to relax. We passed a rambling farm with ornate silos and speculated at what a magnificent inn it could be. We laughed and talked and scouted out remote antique shops and yard sales.

In a non-descript garage I found a beautiful ten-piece Limoge dresser set including little boxes for powder and pearls and trays for hair pins, a hand mirror, an atomizer and a wee bud vase all decorated with hand painted violets and ribbons. The lady of the house wanted $75 for the whole set. All I had with me was $75 and I was reluctant to spend it all in one place. As we drove away without the Limoge set I had a strong suspicion that I would regret that decision for the rest of my life.

One of Geoffrey's favorite topics of conversation was the career plan he had carefully mapped out. He had set his goal to become the owner and operator of a five-star restaurant. His plan of action was to work in various food service situations in order to learn all the angles. He was even planning to work for MacDonald's to find out how they managed their remarkable quality and cost controls. I had no such specific plan for my life. I had decided to take things as they came and see what was around the next bend. Geoffrey and I couldn't seem to agree on which of us had a more realistic approach to life.

We returned from our holiday to a tempest. Mary Hart was faced with a stack of requests for the following weekend off. A concert of epic proportions was planned in White Lake, NY. It was billed as "Woodstock: Three Days of Peace and Music". All the biggest names and the hottest bands were going to perform back to back and 'round the clock. Everyone wanted to go, and, somehow, everyone had gotten tickets. At roll call Mrs. Smith herself came through the Main Dining Room doors to address the situation. Her considered decision was that no one would be given the weekend off in order to avoid favoritism.

Kirsten was the first one to her feet. She carefully folded her apron, walked up to Mrs. Smith, calmly looked her in the eye and said: "In that case, I quit!" And she walked out. Waiters, waitresses and bus boys followed Kirsten's lead and within ten minutes the Main Dining Room crew had shrunk by half.

Mrs. Smith's jaw tightened and she stormed into the kitchen looking for Chef Horne. Leo Ruth and Walter pushed aside the pile of cast off aprons and followed her.

Mr. Ruth returned minutes later to inform the remaining waitresses that the Antebellum Weekend meals would be served buffet style.

But the employee crisis was not the only tempest brewing. A weather pattern far to our south was beginning to look like it could become a hurricane. And a hurricane could spell disaster for the resort industry. At the slightest rumor of a hurricane, guests could be expected to immediately change their vacation plans by checking out or canceling long-standing reservations. We began to watch the weather charts carefully.

As the former employees pulled out of the parking lot headed for Woodstock, the weathermen were officially calling the depression a hurricane—a gusty lady named Camille, aimed right for the Mississippi coast.

A few guests did check out and head for home, but Mississippi seemed so far away that most people paid little attention.

The menus for the Saturday evening Antebellum Dinner had already been printed in the on-site print shop. Presenting the offerings in a buffet setting took some fast thinking. Corn Pone, Boneless Breast of Chicken a la Plantation and Carpet Bagger Blackstone Salad were laid out beside the Confederate States Desserts, which included "Assorted Cookies, Picaninny". I was amazed, once again, that management would condone such a silly and offensive name for an innocent dessert like cookies. But no one else seemed to notice or complain.

Despite the rain that came in. Despite reports of terrible destruction on the Gulf Coast. Despite the fact that half the dining room staff had gone to Woodstock to camp out in the rain and mud. Despite all of this, the Antebellum Dinner was a fabulous success. Guests wore their most elaborate finery that evening. The Smiths had brought in a costume rental organization to afford guests the opportunity to live the evening to the fullest. One of my guests came to dinner in a Confederate officer's uniform complete with a wooden sword that caught on a tablecloth and threatened to dump four place settings at his feet. He managed to untangle the sword and asked me to store it in the umbrella rack in the lobby. Mrs. Smith herself glided through the lobby in a glamorous gown closely resembling a well-padded Scarlet O'Hara.

Sunday morning Mrs. Smith again addressed the diminished staff. She anticipated an influx of Woodstock returnees asking for their jobs back, but she was bound and determined never to allow them to set foot on her property again. She informed us that it was our good fortune that one of the inns down the seacoast was ending their season early and we could expect members of their staff to be joining us. We were also asked to call or write anyone we knew who might be willing to join the staff for the remainder of the season. I promptly composed a letter to my entire college sorority. Within a few days Lynn from New Jersey and Brigitte from Ohio were on their way to Portsmouth. I was rewarded with a small finders fee in my next paycheck.

CHAPTER 18

Wedding Cake

August weddings at the Wentworth were just as charming as the June weddings–and just as lavish. I drew the lucky straw to work a Sunday afternoon celebration/reception of a wedding ceremony that had taken place the evening before on Star Island.

Star Island was the largest island in the Isles of Shoals and accessible only by boat. A hotel and church conference center dominated the island and generations of summer conference-goers had either met one another there or had fond memories of the place. The couple had opted to be married in the tiny stone chapel in a very private and personal candlelight ceremony. I knew the chapel. It was perched on the highest point of Star Island with open ocean to the east and vistas of the mainland to the west. The windows could be barricaded against gale winds by heavy in-ward swinging shutters. The pews were ancient pine boards with initials carved here and there and at the front of the chapel stood a hand-hewn pulpit. On the walls were wooden sconces in the form of outreaching crosses from which lanterns could be hung to light evening services. The wedding ceremony must have been very special.

The reception, however, was undoubtedly the creation of the bride's mother. 150 elite guests were expected in the Ball Room. The Ball Room opened on three sides onto the broad veranda that wrapped the hotel, and on most days the ocean breezes kept the room very comfortable. This particular Sunday afternoon was quite different. The air was hot and heavy and was probably fed by the storm systems associated with Hurricane Camille. The humidity clung to my skin. Overhead fans did their best to move the heavy air around. Very few places in the hotel were air-conditioned. The grand old hotels were built before such modern conveniences.

There was a bar set up near four sets of French doors that opened off an entry corridor. Table centerpieces had been raised from each tabletop by mirrored columns creating fragrant sky-high masterpieces which allowed guests to see and talk with one another without looking through a forest of flower and fern. Sandy Smith was once again the mastermind of every detail. She assigned tables to everyone but asked me to attend to a special matter.

Apparently the heat and humidity were expected to put the five-story wedding cake in peril and I was assigned to guard the confection. The Wentworth baker conferred with me as to what I should do if anything began to slide. He assured me that wooden dowels had been inserted between the layers to reinforce the cake but he gave me a collection of wedges to prevent slippage if any of the layers began to move. He also left me with a walky-talky radio that would connect us should disaster appear imminent. He would be guarding a similar cake at a wedding just down the hill at The Ship.

I took my charge very seriously but tried not to be obvious as to what my duty was. I moved silently from place to place visually lining up the horizontal lines of the cake with the windows. As the guests arrived, everything seemed stable. My cake was true and trim. Finally, when the wedding party appeared everyone was seated and the meal began.

The other waiters and waitresses cleared the appetizers and proceeded to serve the main course. I moved in sync with their movements to avoid being obvious. Still the cake remained level. I was grateful that the bride's family had decided not to have children at this wedding as I could just imagine a wee finger sampling the frosting and creating a landslide.

The next test was the cake cutting ceremony itself. I hovered behind the cake trying not to get close enough to be caught in a Kodak moment. As the bride made the first cut, everything stayed in place, and I realized I was holding my breath. Then the groom cut into the cake, and I felt a shudder go through the whole structure as the knife grazed one of the wooden support dowels. I froze! I could see a slight wrinkle in the frosting on the second tier. The bride fed the groom; the groom fed the bride and both were civilized enough not to get into a cake mashing contest as I had seen at some weddings. I prayed no one would bump against the table. My eye lined up the second tier with the window–it was definitely beginning to sag. I couldn't see how my wedges were going to help if the cake was crumbling under its own weight.

Once the bride and groom were seated we would be free to roll the cake table into the service room in order to cut it up for the guests. Two bus boys who had been assigned to roll the cake out had been watching closely and all three of us were wide-eyed as the cake began to shift. As the attention of the guests was redirected to the head table, the bus boys stepped up to the cake table. I put the wedges down and plunged my hands into the thick white frosting of tier #2. The bus boys began pushing the table with me walking beside it as I physically held the cake together. We turned the corner into the service room just as tier one and tier two lifted off in my hands and the little bride and groom figurine pitched forward. Sandy Smith caught the ornament and helped me ease the cake pieces onto the counter. We looked at each other triumphantly and, after washing my hands thoroughly, we began to cut the cake into serving pieces.

CHAPTER 19

Rye-On-the-Rocks and Breakfast

The crisp perfection of caring for the hotel guests that had hallmarked the earlier weeks of the summer season seemed to have slacked off. The heat and humidity of August took its toll and the staff was becoming worn down. The Woodstock weekend had left staff shortages in all departments. New hires were never trained as thoroughly as we had been and the protocol that created a smooth working relationship between the kitchen and the wait staff was strained. Tempers were short and everyone suffered.

One afternoon Geoffrey, Cher and I decided to ease the heat and the tension with an afternoon drive down the coast to Rye. The Isles of Shoals were clearly visible against an azure sky and the ocean air felt cooler in Rye than in New Castle where a blanket of humidity had enshrouded the Wentworth for over a week.

Our leisurely drive brought us to a popular watering hole overlooking the rocky shore–Rye-On-The-Rocks! A lively crowd of locals, summer vacationers and college kids had the place hopping, singing along with the juke box and tripping over one another as they replenished their drinks. We joined the fun and the bartender suggested we try the daily special: Singapore Slings. All over the room people were sipping tall, frosty pink concoctions. It seemed like the thing to do! We had agreed to have just one, but the luscious drinks slid down so easily that we began to loose track of just how many we'd had. By the time

Geoffrey gave the high sign to head for home we were all spinning in a pink haze.

We squeezed into the MG and headed for home. We were feeling no pain and singing at the top of our lungs when the car began to skid. We had come into a hairpin turn too fast and the little car began to spin like a carnival ride…a 360-degree turn! Miraculously we came to a halt in the middle of the road, unharmed and upright. All three of us were instantly sober. We exchanged a long look that froze my heart. None of us wanted to verbalize the obvious. Very slowly and very deliberately Geoffrey shifted into gear and we drove back to Sagamore in silence. Something in the back of my mind wanted to repeat the rosary…but I wasn't Catholic and I didn't know it. I sensed that Cher was repeating it for all of us.

Alone in my room I washed my face, stared in the mirror, then laid on my cot with my eyes fixed on the ceiling. I was too afraid to think about what had just happened–what COULD have happened. My life seemed very precious and very fragile in that moment. I would very much have welcomed the warmth and safety of my mother's lap!

Breakfast was always a bracing start to each morning at Wentworth-By-The-Sea. A fleet of room service carts was lined up for duty in a caged area off The Zoo. Certain waiters did nothing but room service and were tipped handsomely. The hotel was slow to pick up on "equal opportunity" in regards to the room service opportunities. Female waitresses NEVER took meals to guests' rooms.

In the Main Dining Room we never knew what mood the guests would be in. The one thing that was fairly certain was that everyone would be looking for a cup of robust, freshly brewed coffee. The coffee was brewed in huge stainless steel vats that stood three feet high. We replenished our Pyrex coffee pots from a bank of three of these vats and kept them warm on small heaters in strategically located coffee stations throughout the Main Dining Room. We kept white lids on regular coffee and orange lids on the decaff. Piping hot water was always on tap for tea.

We set our tables with sunny yellow and white striped napkins, made certain every bloom in our centerpieces was fresh, slid delicate white doilies under crocks of raspberry jam and orange marmalade, and piled fresh, warm breakfast breads into baskets.

Most guests began their meal with juice or fruit. We offered an array of melons–Honeydew, Casaba, Crenshaw and, naturally, Canta-loupe. Each was garnished with a wedge of lemon and a sprig of fresh mint. Grapefruit halves were carefully prepared by the pantry crew who pre-cut each section so demure guests would not have to wrestle with unruly grapefruit pulp. This also gave them an opportunity to de-seed each orb. These we garnished with maraschino cherries and served with special grapefruit spoons. There were berries served with wee pitchers of heavy cream; bananas sliced just before serving to prevent even a hint of browning; applesauce topped with a shake of cinnamon sugar and a slice of crisp red apple on the side; oranges peeled and sliced and served in footed compote dishes. One of my guests would have a shot of brandy over his oranges each morning. Pitchers of juice nestled in crushed ice waited for us to pour: orange, grapefruit, apple, cranberry, tomato, prune and a mystery concoction called "Mixed Fruit Juice" that was, in fact, the dregs of each pitcher poured together and chilled. We filled the juice glasses in the kitchen and presented them on tiny under-liners lined with doilies.

Pancakes and waffles were offered. And French Toast made from thick slabs of homemade bread dunked in an egg/cream/nutmeg bat-ter and sizzled in the deep fryer for a perfect five seconds to crisp up, yet not retain any grease. These luscious slabs were served up with a shake of powdered sugar, a small heated carafe of real maple syrup and strips of crisp bacon. As an alternative to the syrup there was always a sauce of fresh strawberries available with a dollop of whipped cream. Some mornings warmed fruit compote was available as a sauce. Fresh peaches with ginger was my personal favorite.

Fried eggs, omelets, Eggs Benedict and poached eggs were cooked to order. Scrambled eggs were pre-cooked and served from heater trays. The eggs on top were fluffy, yellow and delicious. As the heated trays sat, however, the lower layers of scrambleds took on the greenish tint that must have inspired Dr. Seuss. Sheered eggs were popped under the broiler and we had to be very careful to pick up the dishes with a hand towel. Sheered eggs looked like fried eggs cooked in round individual au gratin dishes under the broiler. The bane of my existence, however, was boiled eggs. Along one wall in the kitchen were a half dozen egg boilers that looked like something out of a torture catalog. Metal baskets held one or two eggs and the attached chain lowered the eggs into boiling water below. A timing device automatically reeled in the baskets creating soft-boiled or hard-boiled eggs. Somehow the timers never quite worked and we had to stand guard until the eggs emerged from their frothy hot-water bath.

Toast, English muffins and bagels were sliced and placed on a conveyor belt that disappeared into a giant toasting oven, dropping them out the other side next to a pan of melted butter that was applied with a small basting brush. Every now and then something got caught on the toaster conveyor and thick clouds of acrid smoke filled the area. It was also difficult to tell which English muffin belonged to whom after they disappeared into the cavern of the toaster. I watched girls fight over custody of a slice of rye or a blackened bagel.

Bacon and sausages, ham and corned beef hash were all available, as well as breakfast steak, smoked salmon and kippered herring.

With all the before mentioned to choose from, it always surprised me when someone ordered oatmeal or cold cereal. We offered individual boxes of the classics: Corn Flakes, Rice Krispies, Cherrios, Raisin Bran and Shredded Wheat. Sometimes a child would order Sugar Pops or Frosted Flakes, and even they would magically materialize from the depths of the pantry. At Wentworth-By-The-Sea even cold cereal took on a gourmet look served in pretty china bowls with a plump strawberry or mint sprig on the side accompanied by crystal pitchers of thick cream.

After the morning meal every table was reset with fresh linen, each piece of silver checked and re-checked for tarnish and every third day Mrs. Hackney changed all the centerpieces. Flowers that were still viable found their way into the employee dorms to live out their remaining decorative lives in Dixie Cup vases.

CHAPTER 20

Leanne's Near Conquest

Sagamore became party central from lunchtime forward. Our housemother had long since thrown up her hands in frustration and even an unexpected visit from Mrs. Smith was no longer cause for hysteria.

Leanne had been saving her tips to get her teeth fixed. Waitressing for a living does not provide dental benefits. Her small stash was burning a hole in her pocket and she came back to our room one afternoon with a huge cardboard box containing all the components of an elaborate stereo system. So much for the dentist! Her rationale was that she would now be able to generate enough background distraction that Mandy and I would not mind if she brought home her nightly conquests. After all, Kirsten's former bed now created a 3-foot barrier between her bed and ours. Leanne figured that was privacy enough. We had been aware of Leanne's companions slipping out the back door as we came in the front on several occasions, but the arrival of the stereo seemed to bode a new way of life in our room.

The ranks of the waitresses were strengthened by new arrivals almost every day. Two sisters arrived from the midwest accompanied by their two dogs. Sweetie was a little mutt with a lot of Beagle in her. Polar Bear was a big white Samoyed in dire need of a bath and a good combing. The dogs became the Sagamore mascots.

Within days of Leanne's stereo enhancement, the empty bed in our room was filled by my college pal, Lynn, who arrived from New Jersey to finish out the summer. Lynn was a worldly-wise lass with a hearty laugh and a spirit of adventure. Huddling over beer the afternoon she arrived, Mandy and I filled her in on the summer so far. Lynn was rolling on the floor laughing before we finished. She had been anticipating a change of pace but she had no idea what she was getting into. We speculated about what Leanne would do next.

We didn't have to wait long to find out. The weekly theme was St. Patrick's Day in August. Shamrocks and green carnations decked the tables and a bartender invented a Leering Leprechaun Potion. Irish Aer Lingus provided special menus and a free trip to the Emerald Isle to be awarded to a lucky winner at the Saturday evening Gala Party. Again, the menu boasted oddly named offerings such as Mrs. Murphy's Irish Potato Soup, Irish Lamb Stew Killarney, Fried Oysters Finn MacCool and Shamrock Key Lime Pie.

One of my families for the week had brought together cousins from Newport, Rhode Island and Washington DC to vacation at the Wentworth. I became great buddies with Susie, a third grader, and her cousin Page after I created an especially gooey hot fudge sundae for them in a huge serving dish. We called it the Prudential Center Sundae. Their cousin DeeDee was 13 and had, like so many before her, lost an eye to Corby. He had quickly learned the fine art of flattering the guests, flashing a wink and a smile in the right direction, yet keeping himself at arms length. The fact that he seemed to evaporate after each meal despite DeeDee's efforts to find him made him even more mysterious. DeeDee's vacation would have been perfectly delightful had Corby been the only diversion, but as it turned out, the 13-year-old won the trip to Dublin. I did a jig in the kitchen after the announcement was made–as if I had a personal stake in the fact that my guest had won the trip.

After dinner I dusted green and white confetti off my tables and re-set for breakfast. Corby was re-setting his station nearby and moaning about missed opportunities. Leanne had her tables set in record time and was sidling up to the inventor of the Leering Leprechaun Potion…none other than the handsome Wright, whom we all knew she had elaborate plans for. Mandy and I exchanged amused glances as we left Leanne leaning seductively against one of The Zoo tables goo gahing over the brilliance Wright had exhibited in creating the evening's beverage. We marveled at how she could make even the plain white evening meal uniform look sexy. Perhaps her uniform was a special version ordered from Frederick's of Hollywood!

A keg party was underway at Sagamore when Mandy and I got home. The keg had been set up on the ledge outside Ally and Sil's room and the cousins became a self-appointed welcoming committee bestowing hugs and kisses and frosty mugs of brew on every new arrival. Couples perched on rocks, reclined on blankets and danced in the shadows. Citronella torches kept the mosquitoes at bay and Polar Bear and Sweetie each had a saucer of Bud in front of them. Ally put her arm around me, handed me a beer and planted a big fake kiss on my forehead as if she were my dearest friend. Sil, meanwhile, heard Geoffrey's MG approaching and headed off to greet him with an equal measure of gushiness. Sagamore certainly was a friendly place!

The Citronella torches did not keep the bugs away for long. Mandy, Geoffrey and I retreated to our room where we plumped pillows on the beds and, from the dark, watched the social phenomena going on outside the window. Every now and then Ally or Sil would pop in to refresh our beer mugs. It was amazing how adeptly Ally was able to land a hearty lip-lock on Geoffrey even as he cuddled next to me. He would shrug innocently and comment on how drunk she was.

After awhile Mandy pulled a blanket over her and fell asleep. Geoffrey and I drifted off soon afterwards and we never noticed when the beat from Leanne's stereo took over and the party music outside subsided.

I awoke with a start as Mandy gently shook my arm. My other arm was numb where it was pinned under Geoffrey.

"Leanne has company!" Mandy hissed in a whisper.

Mandy propped herself up on her elbow and fumbled around trying to find her spectacles. I nudged Geoffrey.

Leanne's bedclothes were certainly thrashing around. We could hear huffing and puffing and small moans above the sounds of Big Brother and the Holding Company.

How long had we been asleep? How long had she been at it? And where was Lynn?

Just then the door crashed opened and Lynn leaned against the door jam, the bright hall light behind her. She was three sheets to the wind! She began to pitch forward into the darkened room as Polar Bear came around the corner to see what the ruckus was about. Lynn stumbled and landed on the foot of Leanne's bed. The thrashing stopped. Polar Bear leaped up, pushing Lynn backwards bestowing huge doggie kisses all over her face. Lynn yelled, pushing the big white dog off and scrambled to her feet. Polar Bear retreated, Lynn found her own bed and fell like a dead weight onto the mattress. From beneath Leanne's quilt the legs of her visitor swung over the edge of the bed. As he tried to sit up, Leanne's hands clawed at his shoulders trying to pull him back. In the reflection of the hall light we recognized the undeniably gorgeous silhouette of Wright! Mandy squealed! I burrowed into my pillow laughing uncontrollably. Lynn had passed out. Wright had been unaware of others in the room until that moment and he was mortified. He wrapped himself in Leanne's quilt, collected his clothes from the floor and lurched out of the room. Leanne was wailing!

CHAPTER 21

Auld Lang Sang

The crisp air at the end of August heralded the final week of the Social Season and there was a sadness in the air. It was as if this was a more definitive ending than simply a checkmark on a calendar. Bellmen still guided guests to their rooms; an art exhibit featuring Marion W. Steele was set up in the Geranium Room; children were shepherded to the harbor-side Kiddy Pool by Miss Flipper and Miss Dolphin; Nino and Helen Settinari taught a jolly group of seniors how to cha cha; and a couple of sailing yachts moored in the harbor as if to enhance the souvenir photographs being taken as the summer slowly slid over the horizon.

The elegance and grandeur of the Wentworth-By-The-Sea lifestyle was fading. Mr. and Mrs. James Barker Smith were getting tired. JBjr and Sandy, the only hope of passing the legacy on, appeared stiff and formal together in public. Separately they shone and they sparkled, but one had to wonder whether there were problems in their little love nest on the knoll above the golf course. Hotel guests no longer stayed for the entire summer, and teenage guests didn't feel they needed Tim Yeager to organize their days. People didn't care whether there was chamber music in the Main Dining Room or dance lessons in the Ballroom, but they were complaining about the lack of air conditioning. Even the staff was different. Pride in serving was a thing of the past. The instinct throughout society in 1969 was to question authority, often blatantly. Even if a waitress knew she should serve from the left and clear from the right, she rarely did it. There was antagonism between the perceived "Haves" (the guests) and the "Have-Nots" (the staff). It was no longer a graceful dance between the classes.

As could be predicted, the final weekend of Social Season was well attended and took on the air of New Years Eve. The final dinner was aptly called Auld Lang Sang. Strip Sirloin, Father Time didn't sound very appealing to me, but then I was never a fan of aged beef.

One of my Labor Day Weekend tables consisted of four couples from Medford, Massachusetts who were up to play golf, dine and drink and make merry. I never did figure out which wife was attached to which husband.

A second table was occupied by yearly Labor Day visitors from Jamaica Plain boasting several generations from the stylish grandmother to two-year-old Richard who was a hellion with a penchant for throwing food.

The Rocco and DiNapoli families had been at the Wentworth for the Fourth of July and always returned, with grandchildren in tow, for the close of the summer.

Miss Slattery and Miss Devlin were wonderful, intellectual dears who enjoyed rocking on the veranda, exchanging political views with other guests and perusing the antique shops of the area.

The Drea sisters had been back three or four times during the summer and although they were very proper and somewhat fussy about their needs, they were delightful ladies, representative of the clientele that the Wentworth had always catered to. They enjoyed high tea wearing white gloves and their best pearls.

After the Auld Lang Sang Dinner we packed away the green service plates and crystal finger bowls. They would not be needed during convention season. I silently wondered whether they would ever come out of storage again.

The Round Robin had an over stock of ice cream and we were encouraged to help diminish the supply. Mandy had always wanted to try a chocolate ice cream soda with lime sherbet and this was her opportunity. I doubt that she (or anyone else) ever ordered that combination again.

Labor Day Weekend always saw the departure of droves of guests as well as staff. I planned to work the Fall Convention Season until I returned to college. The powers that be had decided to assemble those of us remaining, in more proximal living quarters. At Sagamore, we were preparing to move once again. Mandy and I found that we were heading back to Colonial Cottage.

The last night of Labor Day Weekend most of the departing staff members had already packed their cars, turned in their uniforms and picked up their final paychecks. The rooms at Sagamore were looking bare and there was nothing to do but fill them with music and dancing and an all night final fling.

Someone acquired a galvanized trash barrel and someone else provided a grape-juice punch base. From there we all contributed any and all liquor that we had in our possession. Wine was also acceptable in the mixture, but beer and malt beverages were nixed. We stirred the brew, added a bucket of ice and created the most potent punch of the summer. And it tasted yummy!!

It seemed as if the entire population of the seacoast was at Sagamore. Three Dog Night blared and as we danced, jostling each other, no one cared that we were ankle deep in punch. There was a lull in the music and a crowd of us tumbled onto the unmade cots. I found myself half on top of one bus boy and cheek-to-cheek with Corby. Not only did he look good up close, but he smelled good, too! I could feel the fuzz of his 16-year-old beard on my cheek. Geoffrey was rolling around with Ally, Sil and Tanya and no one seemed to care whether the music started again or not. But the music did start and the bus boys were on their feet pulling everyone else up with them. Geoffrey found me in the crowd and pulled me close. What an interesting summer we'd had! It wasn't long before Ally nuzzled her way through the crowd and somehow I found myself dancing with someone else. Ally maneuvered Geoffrey towards the punch barrel and, as she ran her hands up and down his back, they refilled their glasses. The vision made something snap in my brain. With a singular motion I let fly the glass in my hand aimed at the wall directly beside Ally's head. The glass shattered into a million pieces and Ally let out a scream. The party noise went silent for a split second. When everyone felt certain that Ally had not been mortally wounded, the party continued. Ally began to cry and leaned towards Geoffrey for comfort. He had the wisdom to step away and return to my side where he remained quite attentively for the rest of the night.

The next day Sagamore was mothballed and all of our gear was transported back to Colonial Cottage. In honor of the grand move, Cher found a huge box of crepe paper decorations left over from the Fourth of July. We proceeded to trim the railings, downspouts and porch pillars with red, white and blue streamers. The dorm looked very festive as we headed for the Main Dining Room to serve the evening meal. Unfortunately, during that evening, a light rain fell on New Castle, New Hampshire and all the streamers bled into the white railings, pillars and downspouts of Colonial Cottage. We were all reprimanded and a team of maintenance guys had to come over to repaint the places that had been stained.

CHAPTER 22

Ebbings and Endings

The first convention after Labor Day was a group called PIMA. We saw their banners and their tee shirts and their baseball caps everywhere, yet none of us knew who these PIMA's really were.

The PIMA's enjoyed buffet brunch each day, a series of golf and tennis events and scenic tours of the area. On the final night of their stay, a long head table was set up along the front wall of the Main Dining Room. This was their big awards banquet and those of us who had been serving them during the week finally found out that PIMA stood for Paper Industry Manufacturers Association.

Because so many of our cohorts had left right after Labor Day, it was easier to work in teams of two as we could cover more tables. Executing the detailed pampering of Social Season was impossible, but the convention folks didn't expect it anyway.

My teammate was a waiter named Randy. He was a newcomer...a friend of a friend of a staff member who had been recruited after the Woodstock exodus. He had arrived about the same time as Bridgett, my sorority sister. The Bridgett I knew at college was very pretty, very proper and very much aware of her image and reputation. The Bridgett that arrived at the Wentworth was an entirely different young lady. She and Randy had been em-broiled in an animal magnetism that began the minute they laid eyes on one another. Randy was having a grand time, and I would hazard a guess that Bridgett was too, but there was an unspoken message that hung in the air whenever I was around her. I was quite certain that if, after we were back on campus, I breathed even a hint of what the summertime Bridgett was about, she would slit my throat as I slept. So I quietly ignored the rutting couple.

Conventions came and went quickly. They generally lasted only three or four days and depending upon the number of people attending, there could be two or three conventions going on simultaneously as the Wentworth could accommodate up to 500 guests.

The national convention of a Greek fraternity overlapped with the PIMA group, followed by the Massachusetts Bankers Association. Some groups held workshops and seminars, while others were there simply to fraternize. There were always golf or tennis tournaments, historic tours of Portsmouth, excursions to the New Castle Coast Guard Station and tour boats headed for the Isles of Shoals. There was rarely a

convention that passed up a lobster bake and most ended their stay with a formal awards dinner complete with speeches.

The Massachusetts Bankers Association requested the traditional Convention Dessert Parade. After dinner the lights would dim, a drum roll would sound and all of us would march single file around the Main Dining

Room each carrying a battery-powered, lighted globe on our shoulder topped with a little platform on which perched the dessert of the evening.

The parade of waitresses finally came to stop at the head table and we ceremoniously presented our offerings to the onlookers.

One afternoon a group of convention wives asked me to join them as they went exploring. We ended up at the Wentworth-Coolidge Mansion on Little Harbor Road in Portsmouth. The oddly shaped 42-room mansion dominated a point of land visible from the back veranda of the hotel. Obviously, Wentworths had been in the area for a very very long time. The mansion had been the home of Benning Wentworth, the first royal governor in New Hampshire in the mid 1700's. He had constructed it by joining several smaller buildings together, some dating back to 1695, to form the present building. The tour guide was well versed in the history of every piece of furniture, every scrap of wall covering and every hearth throughout the mansion. We began at the back of the manse where the servants' quarters would have been. It was interesting that the kitchen was built for French cooking with deep cooking wells for making soups and stews and sauces…very fancy for the day! Our little group moved forward to the more formal front of the house where carriages of visitors would have been received. The main dining room had the illusion of being oval because of built-in buffets in each corner. Two female torsos resembling ships figureheads flanked the fireplace in that room. I speculated that the local talent in 1741 only knew how to carve figureheads. Undoubtedly the governor had intended the fireplace to have a Greek goddess look to it, but those Greek stonecutters just weren't available to do the job that century.

The best part of the tour was our guide's dramatic recitation of Longfellow's poem "Lady Wentworth". Apparently old Benning W. decided to end his widower-hood on his 60th birthday. While hosting a lavish dinner in honor of himself, he summoned his 20 year old house-keeper, Martha Hilton, and commanded the local reverend to marry them on the spot. One of those winter/spring marriages! When the good governor died, his entire estate was left to his youthful bride who remarried within two months.

Most afternoons I spent with Geoffrey. He was already looking towards the next step in his plan. He had decided to travel to Fort Lauderdale after the Wentworth closed in October to spend the winter working at the Lauderdale Beach Hotel. My plan was to return to college and finish my senior year–the culmination of a few false starts and some extra time seeking my BA degree. The fork in the road was coming upon us quickly. We had no time for flirtations with other staff members. We immersed ourselves in the warmth and familiarity of each other…laughing, loving, talking, dreaming, yet both of us fully aware that our time together was short.

Some evenings Geoffrey would cook dinner for me at Colonial Cottage and we would "borrow" place settings and linens from the Main Dining Room, candles form the Avenida Terrace and Leanne's stereo to provide low background music. Geoffrey and I had jointly purchased the Blood, Sweat and Tears album with "our song" on it:

"You made me so very happy; I'm so glad you came into my life."

We played it over and over again. No mention was made of which of us was to get custody of the album.

We took time to visit Geoffrey's parents in Hampton. His mother undoubtedly interpreted my continued high-profile in her son's life as hope that she might one day have me for a daughter-in-law.

We visited Jackson in Amesbury once again and I felt that despite the inevitability of our fork in the road, Geoffrey was pulling me as close to him and his life as he could. Perhaps it was an attempt to create a portal into another chapter down the road. Those "roads that diverge in a yellow wood" must have side-shoots that potentially cross again.

The Rotarians Fall Enclave checked in and engulfed the entire resort with their activities and programs. During the Rotarians' stay Leanne packed her leopard skin luggage, collected her final paycheck and waited on our porch for the young man she described as her "hometown honey".

A shiny black Excalibur rumbled across the Wentworth drawbridge and drew quite a bit of attention. Leanne explained to the bellhops that an Excalibur was a replica of an old Dusenburg with a modern day Corvette engine. Her knight in shining armor was the driver! His car was so impressive that most of us hardly noticed him at all. I only remember that he had a moustache and bad teeth. He piled Leanne's luggage into the car, swept her off her feet, tucked a lap robe around her (leopard skin, of course) and they were off to seek their fortune and, hopefully, a dentist.

There was a textile convention. Next, a group of engineers arrived and brought in a stripper for their last night banquet. Mrs. Smith was horrified. Finally, there was an evening reunion of some elderly Phillips Exeter Academy grads.

Then it was my turn to move on.

I worked the Exeter reunion my final evening. It was humorous to see old men still holding grudges over long ago football rivalries.

The next morning I bundled up all my uniforms and Geoffrey drove me to the Portsmouth Laundromat to wash them all. I knew the Valet Shop would clean everything anyway, but I prided myself in the condition of my uniforms and I wanted to turn them in crisp and spotless, with every button neatly in place. While the uniforms were churning in their suds, Geoffrey and I indulged in waffles at Jarvis's Restaurant across the ally. Waffles were a favorite of Geoffrey's!

While we ate we speculated about the number of fires that summer. Were they all accidents? Was Pebble Beach truly brought down by an iron someone left on? Or was someone trying to run the Smiths out of business? Would the dorms be rebuilt?

Back at Colonial Cottage, Mandy helped me pack and I discovered that I was leaving with a lot more than I had arrived with. I had picked up new clothes with each paycheck, a brass birdcage, and a piece of Lamberton Scammell china and a whole summer's worth of Wentworth-By-The-Sea memories. My heart was full of Geoffrey and Mandy. I visited the Valet Shop one more time to return my uniforms; I stopped by Mary Hart's office to turn in my key and pick up my final paycheck; I swung by the front office to shake Mr. and Mrs. Smith's hands and thank them; and I jogged across the causeway to say goodbye to Kay. Joseph was at Kay's and gave me a big hug that started my misting eyes overflowing. I contemplated finding Corby to wish him well, but he had tucked his address in my pocket the night before and I was quite sure we would be in touch.

I was a bit whimpery and red-eyed through all these ebbings and endings, but once seated in Daddy's station wagon I completely broke down. We drove past the grand old Wentworth-By-The-Sea and slowed to let some putting green people across the road. I looked back at Kay's island as we crossed the bridge and wound past the perfect green vastness of the golf course. My summer of 1969 had been a memorable one and we had indeed: "Flashed across the summer scene like a shooting star. Crowding a thousand exciting things into the short bright months."

CHAPTER 23

And the Years Went By

And the years went by…

As for the players, JBjr and Sandy did get divorced. The absence of Sandy's strong, firm hand at the helm pretty much ended any hope that the Smith dynasty at the Wentworth would continue into another generation.

After operating the hotel for nearly 35 years, the elder Smiths sold it to a Swedish company in 1980. The Swedes kept it afloat for two more years but in 1982 Wentworth-By-The-Sea closed it's doors–probably forever. James Barker Smith, Sr. went into a nursing home and died in 1990. Margaret Smith was moved by her son, JBjr, to a nursing home in Georgia where she died in 1995. They lived long enough to see a vast portion of the hotel bulldozed in 1989.

Corby grew up straight and strong and smart and earned himself an appointment to West Point. And, yes, our paths did cross again.

Mandy returned to Sarasota to write her own 500 page novel…probably one to rival this one.

Geoffrey's dreams came true. He acquired the skills he wanted, opened his own restaurant just outside Ithaca, NY and added a vineyard to his holdings. I helped write the manual by which he trained his waitresses. One of the crowning glories of his career was the night the James Barker Smiths came to his establishment for dinner.

Leanne married her Excalibur boyfriend, became a respected nursery school teacher and an animal rights activist vehemently opposed to the use of fur for personal adornment.

And as for me, I drifted back to Wentworth-By-The-Sea over and again for several years. I was addicted to the place! I always knew I had a job and a place to live waiting for me. One season I arrived in New Castle in March, moved in with Kay and helped open the hotel for the following season. Each time I returned, Wentworth-By-The-Sea had lost a little more of her luster. It was breaking my heart. The last time I turned in my uniform and room key was in 1975. But in the summer of 2000 that key came 'round again.

I discovered the eBay auction site on the internet and began collecting whatever became available that preserved a little bit of the Wentworth-By-The-Sea legend. On eBay I acquired postcards from every era, commemorative glassware, an ashtray and some old menus. I also e-mailed other regular bidders to determine their interest in the old gal. This group of face-less cyberspace contacts were Wentworth-By-The-Sea aficionados, ready to commit a couple of bucks to a 1911 postcard or duel to the death over a menu from 1958.

On June 29, 2000, I was making my regular check of what was available, and my eyes fell upon an interesting item: a Wentworth-By-The-Sea key. The description read: "We have three of these keys so we'll put one on eBay for all you New Castle natives who have moved away and need a touch of home. Key tag says 5 Col. Cottage, over a post office box address in Portsmouth, N.H. I bought these in a lot with other keys that also said the Wentworth by the Sea, and the person who brought them in said they were from the Wentworth. These keys apparently were to the cottages at the Wentworth. Large brass key is 3 1/2 inches long." Victory Antiques of Portsmouth, N.H, offered it.

I was startled by the description. It sounded like the key to Mandy's and my room. I scrolled down to the photograph of the brass skeleton key and found that it was, indeed, MY KEY!!! Just after midnight that first day, I placed my bid and began the long, suspenseful wait until July 9, 2000 at 19:14:50 PDT when the auction would be over. I e-mailed the others who were likely to bid against me telling them that this was the Holy Grail for me. I also contacted Barbara Metzler at Victory

Antiques and got descriptions of the other two keys. "ryeman" got the key to Room 240 which would have been a room on the top floor in the wing that extended off the back of the main building overlooking the clay tennis courts. Upper echelon employees lived in those rooms–perhaps the tennis pro, the social director or Miss Flipper. "vzteacher" got the key to Room 318. That would also have been an employee room and, interestingly enough, was the housekeepers' dorm area in the center tower over the port cochere.

And so I waited and received daily encouragement from the people who were watching the auction with me. The days ticked by! I would look at the key every once in awhile and was relieved that no one was bidding against me. Not until July 2nd! Out of nowhere came an unknown bidder known as "zin". "zin" had no prior history of bidding on eBay. Six times "zin" went to bat and bid the key up to $31.50. By the end of the day, with my fingernails bitten to the quick, I was still the high bidder.

And so I waited! I knew "ryeman", "vzteacher", "eemcgowan", "bluepenguin" and "awesomeannie" were not likely to turn on me. But what about "rwent", "mrpenmark", "djurcik01" or "ryeken"? And then there was the shrewd and dreaded "tadgh" lurking just beyond sight. But Lady Luck was at my side. Despite a torrential downpour that threatened the very electrical life-blood of my computer, the end of the auction came, and I had triumphed!!!!

The key was mine once again.

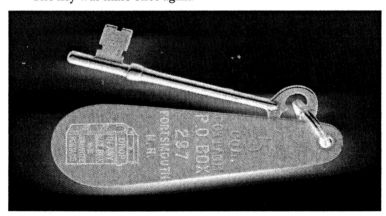

The key sat on my dressing table for a few days calling to me. By the summer of 2000 Wentworth-By-The-Sea had become a haunted shell waiting to blow away in the gales of winter. I knew I had to go back one more time. The first week in August I made the pilgrimage. I had no choice. No will!

As I approached the turn onto the Wentworth Road I noted that Ladd's, our mixing-mingling-and-drinking place, is now a mental health center. Bizarre! The ice cream stand is now called "The Ice House" and JBjr's cute cottage at #100 has been renovated. New buildings dot the golf course constructed in compatible architecture that makes them look like they have always been there. The Smith's house on the right by the drawbridge looks hollow. Campbell's Island to the left is dominated by three elaborate Florida-style condominiums in place of the tall fally-down house. The condos rather dwarf Kay's old house. The Ship peers out over the harbor from dark, empty portholes and is badly in need of a drydocking. Just below it, a spectacular marina has burgeoned from the original Ski Shack. Then I came to the remains of the hotel. The Main Dining Room is gone, severed at the etched glass doors and everything from that point on has been razed. The vast kitchens have been torn down and a shadowy outline indicates where the elevator shaft used to be. The guts of the operation where the boilers were housed has also met the wrecking ball. Even the foundation is beginning to shift. The last remaining part of the hotel is completely surrounded by a tall chain link fence. But over the still-standing port cochere, remains the weathered lettering "Wentworth-By-The-Sea", as if the letters themselves are trying to keep the memory alive by clinging to the façade.